www.SaucyRomanceBooks.com/RomanceBooks

Make Me Yours

It's not official till it's official...

"Dean, make me yours..."

That's all Meaghan wants.

The two have always shared a mutual attraction, despite their

upbringings being worlds apart.

Dean is an entitled billionaire with commitment issues.

Meaghan grew up in a deprived neighborhood and now holds a

respectable position in a busy hospital.

Things between them are complicated; not properly together, but

not seeing anyone else.

But things are about to get even more complex.

A new friendship formed between Meaghan and a hunky doctor has Dean brewing with jealousy.

Forcing the two to reassess their situation, can they do what's needed to make what they have work?

Or will Dean's commitment issues force the woman he's always loved into another man's arms?

Find out in this hot new BWWM romance by Cher Etan.

Suitable for over 18s due to steaming hot love making scenes.

Brought to you by Saucy Romance Books - search 'BWWM Club' on Amazon for all our BWWM romance stories.

Get Free Romance eBooks!

Hi there. As a special thank you for buying this book, for a limited time I want to send you some great ebooks completely **free of charge** directly to your email! You can get it by going to this page:

www.saucyromancebooks.com/physical

You can see a the cover of these books on the next page:

www.SaucyRomanceBooks.com/RomanceBooks

ONE LONE COWBOY, ONE WOMAN ON A MISSION...

THE LONE COWBOY

EMILY J

ROCHELLE

IF IT'S MEANT TO BE...

Him

KIMBERLY GREENFORD

...RE MET HIS MATCH?

UCH LASS

...LDING

PLAYER GONNA PLAY?

SHE'S THE ONE HE WANTS
BUT CAN SHE TRUST HIM?

ONE VAMPIRE. ONE COP. ONE LOVE.

VAMPIRES OF CLEARVIEW

J A FIELDING

www.SaucyRomanceBooks.com/RomanceBooks

These ebooks are so exclusive you can't even buy them. When you download them I'll also send you updates when new books like this are available.

Again, that link is:

www.saucyromancebooks.com/physical

ISBN-13: 978-1512385151

ISBN-10: 1512385158

Copyright © 2015 to Cher Etan and SaucyRomanceBooks.com. No part of this book can be copied or distributed without written permission from the above copyright holders.

Contents

www.SaucyRomanceBooks.com/RomanceBooks

Chapter 1

The country club was quiet at six am; only a number of golfers milling around waiting for their caddies. It was Dean's favorite time of day as he milled around waiting for Smith and his father to arrive. They used to be a foursome…before his own father's stroke had rendered him immobile. But they still kept up the tradition – Smith and Jonathan Winchester's way of saying that they were there for him he supposed – and Dean wasn't about to be the one to break it. He needed this; needed the connection to people with whom he could reminisce about a side of his father very few people saw. A hand clapped him on the shoulder and he turned around to see Smith smiling at him.

"Hey," he said.

"Hey man, ready to go?" Smith asked. His father was strolling toward them in conversation with his caddy. He'd had the same one for nigh on twenty years now. He no longer worked at the club but turned up for the game. He was part of the tradition too. Dean sighed, his heart heavy yet soothed by the presence of his friend; his family really, if one wasn't such a stickler for blood. Smith frowned at him.

"What's wrong?" he asked.

Dean looked up at him smiling at how well his friend knew him, "Nothing. The usual." He said and Smith nodded like Dean had made perfect sense.

"How's Poppy?" he asked next, eyes already ready to commiserate.

Dean shrugged, "It's been quiet. Too quiet. She hasn't hounded me once this week about ruining the family name or destroying our lives or giving her a stroke too...its making me tense."

"You think she's up to something?" Smith asked smile widening into a grin.

"Isn't she always?" he replied.

"Could you ask Bella if she's maybe heard anything on the bitch circuit about what my mother and Samantha could be planning?" Dean pleaded.

"What? You don't think the surprise birthday party they threw you was enough?" Smith asked laughing outright. "Oh my God your face – I'll never forget."

"You can laugh...I'm the one who had to deal with the fallout," Dean glared at him, "Although Meaghan was surprisingly cool about it. Didn't so much as freeze me out of her bed or anything."

"Oh, now that there *should* worry you," Smith retorted still snorting with laughter.

Dean shrugged, "Mmm, I don't know, Meaghan knows how I feel about her. And she knows that my mom and Samantha are trying to sabotage us. I don't think she'd willingly fall into one of their traps – she's not stupid."

Smith smiled. "And you guys still in love? The shine hasn't faded from the relationship? It's been six months after all. That's like... four years in dog years," he said tongue in cheek.

Dean looked seriously at him and sighed, "Man, I'm in trouble."

"Why?" Smith asked although he suspected he knew.

"Because this is the real thing," Dean said looking downcast and forlorn.

Smith nodded his head in agreement, "Yeah, it's kinda obvious you got it bad."

"I don't know what to do man," Dean confided.

"Don't know what to do about what?" Jonathan Winchester asked coming up alongside them.

Dean and Smith exchanged sidelong glances and then Smith said, "He's worried about Jeffrey Dad."

"Oh," Jonathan said with a clap on Dean's back. "Jeffrey is one of the toughest men I know Dean, he'll pull through this. You just wait and see."

*****

The object of Dean and Smith's conversation was just arriving for her shift at work. They'd call her in early because of a multi-car accident that had occurred on I-295, whose victims were being brought to the hospital. Meaghan was a bit nervous even though this wasn't her first rodeo; it *was* her first time dealing with an emergency of this magnitude. She knew she would have to think on her feet and react as fast as possible which was just the opposite of her style which consisted of thinking everything through carefully, weighing pros and cons and coming to a decision about how to proceed that way.

As she stepped in the hospital door, the first ambulance was screeching to a halt in front of accidents and emergencies and she hurried to her office to find her coat and wash her hands so she could get to work. The very first person brought in was a child with a broken leg and she was paged to deal with it. After that the day was just one long blur of blood and gore and death. Meaghan didn't think she'd ever worked so hard in her life but for every life that was saved there was one they could do nothing for and Meaghan felt every loss like a personal failure. When all the emergency patients were treated there were still regular patients waiting...it was a long day.

Her phone rang at the end of it and she looked down to see that it was Dean calling her. She stared at the name for a while wondering if she should answer but she was physically and mentally exhausted. There was no way she could summon enough energy to be the girlfriend right now. She barely had enough to declare herself a human being. So she clicked ignore then texted him to say she'd speak to him later, long day, blah blah. She put her phone in her pocket and sighed deeply then started when a cup of coffee appeared before her face held by the most delicate looking pair of hands she'd ever seen. She followed the hands to the face and her eyebrows went up in surprise. It was the new supervisor; Dr… Shelley or something. All the nurses were buzzing in excitement about him and calling him Dr. Sexy. He was a tall distinguished looking man with jet black hair going gray at the temples. His eyes were piercing blue and he tended to pin people down with them. She'd seen doctors lose their ability to speak when Dr Sexy, er, Shelley fixed his eyes on them. And now the same thing seemed to be happening to her.

"I thought you could use this," he said, his deep voice soothing her wounded spirit.

"Thanks," she squeaked not exactly sure why this guy was even speaking to her. They had been introduced at the meeting at which he was presented to them but had hardly exchanged two words since.

"I've been watching you Ms. Leonard," he drawled smiling at her.

Meaghan brows lifted at the 'Ms.'; she wondered if it would be incredibly rude or extremely flirty to say 'that's *Dr* Leonard to you'. She didn't really know how these games were played.

"Why have you been watching me?" she asked instead.

"Because...you're going to make a great surgeon one day," he said fixing her with that stare and making her hand shake. Nerves; it was just nerves.

"Really?" she asked voice higher than usual. Dr. Shelley was a neurosurgeon of really good repute. The hospital was lucky to have him. He'd said he'd wanted to work here because he grew up in Queens. Meaghan had been really surprised to hear that – he certainly did not have the look of any of *her* neighbors...but it also gave her hope. If a fellow Queens resident could reach the heights that Dr. Shelley had then surely she had a chance too.

"Yes. Really. Plus I hear you grew up around here too," he said.

Meaghan stared at him suspiciously, she could be crazy but he really did sound like he was flirting with her. She couldn't remember what the nurses had said about his marital status though...either way; she had a boyfriend so it wouldn't fly. Should she just come right out and say so though or how the fuck did this work?

"I did grow up here. My mother worked as a nurse in this community and she inspired me to go into medicine," she said.

"That's cool. My dad was a mechanic and my mother is a house wife," he informed her.

"Oh," Meaghan said at a loss for how to reply.

"Well anyway, I wanted to compliment you on the exemplary work you did today. First rate. Was this your first crisis situation?" he asked.

"Yes," Meaghan said warmed by his words, "It was…"

Dr. Shelley nodded, "Yes, I know. The first one can be overwhelming. Would you like to sit down to some coffee and talk about it?"

"Yes I would," Meaghan said with relief. She definitely needed to talk to someone about her day and Dr. Shelley would understand her like neither Bain nor Dean would. He had been there; maybe he could give her some useful tips about how to get over the feeling of failure when one of her patients died; or how to cope with being immured in people's shit all day every day and then have to go home and smile at your loved one like everything was alright with the world. When you *knew* how fucked up it really was right this minute, where some kid was dying and you can't save them and you have to put on a brave face and tell their parents that there

was nothing more you could do. It sucked ass.

*****

Dean drew up to the hospital anticipating surprising Meaghan by

taking her home and cooking her dinner. He'd heard about the

accident on I-295 and that patients had been taken to Mt. Sinai. So

he'd called earlier to commiserate but she hadn't picked up and he

knew it had been hard for her. He realized they rarely talked about

the hard things; too many barriers to that, what with his family

drama and their limited time together which he realized was mostly

spent in bed. After his talk this morning with Smith he'd realized he

didn't *really* know how Meaghan felt about the continuous

attempts to sabotage them perpetrated by his mother and his ex-

girlfriend. She always said she was fine with it; that she understood

but maybe...

He pulled into the parking lot just in time to see her sliding into a blue SUV with a tall white older looking guy. The guy drove off and before Dean could think about it, he was following them. They didn't go very far; just to *La Trattoria*, Meaghan's favorite restaurant...the guy handed her out of the car – she was smiling at him – and they walked into the restaurant. Dean vacillated between wanting to drive off right away and wanting to find out who this guy was who *his girlfriend* seemed to have blown him off for. It seemed she wasn't too tired to talk to *him*. He snatched his phone off the console and sent Meaghan a text.

Where are you?

He tapped his foot, waiting anxiously for her reply. Willing her to tell him the truth. She didn't reply for a while and Dean was just contemplating stepping out of the car and going to confront her when his notifications pinged.

I'm at work. See you later?

Dean stared at the text, his eyes burning and his heart beat fibrillating dangerously.

She had lied to him.

Dean leaned back on the head rest of his seat, traitorous thoughts swirling in his head. How many times? How many men? Was any of this real? Was she playing him? So many questions with no answers. Dean tried to calm down, to wait and see but he could feel his heart breaking. He'd risked everything for her and she did...*this*? Before he knew he had decided to do it, Dean was alighting from the vehicle and heading into the restaurant. Luigi was at the maitre d's station speaking with him in low tones. He looked up and saw Dean, and his face lit up with a smile.

"Dean! How nice to see you. Have you come to join Meaghan and her doctor friend?" he asked.

Dean shook his head. "No, I just thought I'd...have a cup of Joe.

Don't tell them I'm here," he tried out a smile for size but didn't

think Luigi was fooled.

"Oh," he said in a tone implying he was drawing his own

conclusions. He extended his arm, indicating that Dean should

follow him and led him to a table from which he had a good view of

Meaghan and her guest; but she couldn't see him. Luigi left him to

his own devices and someone brought him a coffee before long. He

was too busy watching Meaghan interact with the man to notice.

Their conversation seemed extremely intense and Meaghan was

talking a lot. Dean would have given his left arm for a listening

device right now. The white guy leaned forward, not breaking eye

contact with her, and put his hand on top of hers on the table. Dean

almost lost it right there and then. Who the *fuck* was this guy and

what did he think he was doing putting his hand on *Dean's*

girlfriend?? Luigi came by and slid into the seat opposite Dean, temporarily blocking his view of Meaghan. Dean transferred the glare he'd been directing at Meaghan's companion to Luigi.

"You know distrust is the death bringer of relationships," Luigi intoned. "I know that for sure because it's coming between my wife and me."

Dean was not in the mood to be diplomatic. "What's coming between your wife and you is the fact that you're still in love with Bain," he said cuttingly. Luigi had the grace to look shamefaced but then rallied.

"Regardless of that. This is not the way to go about these things," he said. Dean had become a friend so he was allowed to be snippy now and then; especially if he was upset over Meaghan possibly cheating on him. Luigi knew how bad Dean had it. He and Meaghan had eaten at the restaurant many times so Luigi had plenty of opportunity to observe them. Plus he still spoke to Bain, so he knew about all the family drama on Dean's side.

"How would you suggest we 'go about' these things?" Dean's tone was just a little bit snarky.

"Would you like me to find out who he is?" Luigi offered, making Dean feel bad about his rudeness. He thought about it seriously but then found that he wasn't ready to know if Meaghan was cheating and then thinking that Meaghan was aware that Luigi knew about them and surely she wouldn't be flaunting another guy in front of him if she wanted to keep it a secret. So either there was another explanation or...

Dean shook his head, "No don't. I'll wait for her to tell me herself," he said standing up and drawing a bill down on his plate. "I'd be grateful if you didn't mention I was here," he said. Luigi nodded and Dean turned to leave with a muttered thanks.

*****

"So where in Queens did you grow up," Meaghan asked, curious to find out as much of his journey as she could.

"Well I grew up in Queensborough; like I said my dad was a mechanic," he said.

"So why medicine?"

Dr. Shelley shrugged, "Well you know the way boys grow up playing with cars and video games and running outside climbing trees...if they're lucky enough to live in neighborhoods that still have those that is."

Meaghan smiled and nodded.

"Well, I grew up dissecting first Barbie dolls and then insects...the occasional frogs. I wanted to find out how things worked. My mother thought I was gay at first, and then she was afraid I was a serial killer," Dr. Shelley said smiling wryly.

Meaghan laughed. "So what happened? Did she take you to a psychiatrist?"

"No, lucky for me I had a science teacher who recognized my interest for what it was and guided me toward less disturbing ways to satisfy my curiosity about the human body. He was my first and most important mentor. Without him I might not be where I am today."

"Teachers can be great," Meaghan agreed.

"What about you? What's your story?" he asked.

Meaghan shrugged. "I came from the wrong side of the tracks but I wanted to get into the right schools so I applied for a scholarship, played up my disadvantages and gave them perfect grades. I had a great teacher to help me do that too. From there it wasn't too difficult to get into Dalton and from Dalton to Yale. The rest as they say is history."

"Wow, you attended Dalton School? That's...impressive." Dr. Shelley was nodding his head at her and smiling his approval and Meaghan couldn't help but feel glowy inside.

"Yeah I did. Anyway, it was a great ride and my mother was very supportive. Lonely though; it wasn't like I could come home and discuss my day with the neighbor's kid," she twisted her lips as she said.

"I'm familiar with that problem. My neighbor's kid was selling pot by the time he was twelve. A real entrepreneurial type – really made my life difficult because one, I was white, and two, I actually took school seriously."

Meaghan laughed and nodded, "My neighbor's kid was pregnant for the second time by her fifteenth birthday. She dropped out of school I think, not sure though. She thought I had airs so she didn't talk to me much."

Dr. Shelley laughed and nodded his head. "Yeah. Good times", he said. He lifted his coffee cup to her in salute and she returned the gesture. They drank, feeling more at ease and smiling at each other.

"I have this youth development project that I run back home. We do mentorship, inner city rescue and we have a clinic where we exchange dirty needles for clean ones every other Saturday. I'd really love it if you would think about joining us," he said.

Meaghan perked up. "What? You're joking. I'd *love* to do that. Hell the reason I'm working at the Queens clinic is to give back to my community. Don't know when I'll find the time though."

"Well if it helps, we have some paid positions for clinicians. It comes with a good medical plan too; though I imagine you're on Obamacare already? Anyway, I know you work locum at some other hospital so instead of that you could come to us hmm? It could work?" Dr. Shelley suggested.

Meaghan opened her mouth to say something but her heart was too full. After such a shitty day to be offered such a thing was…well it had come just in time.

"I accept," she breathed smiling.

"Don't you want to come check us out first? See what we do? Maybe ask how much the pay is?" Dr. Shelley teased.

"Okay then I accept subject to finding out all of the above Dr. Shelley," she said grinning.

"Brilliant. I just know we will work well together Meaghan Leonard, M.D. I really look forward to having you on our team. We work with a whole lot of young upcoming doctors but we also have seasoned professionals. Dr. Ben Carson came by just last month to give a talk," he told her.

"Really? Wow. Tell me more," Meaghan said eagerly.

"Okay but first I have one request," Dr. Shelley said.

"What?" Meaghan asked.

"Call me Conrad."

Meaghan smiled, "Got it. Conrad. Now tell me more."

Conrad lifted his hand to the waiter to indicate they were ready for more coffee. And then he told her everything there was to know about his project. Meaghan listened with rapt attention getting more and more excited to be part of something so practical yet with the potential to make such a difference. She couldn't wait to tell Bain all about it.

*****

Bain walked into *La Trattoria* that night to have dinner before heading to the strip club to catch his boyfriend's show. He was feeling particularly out of sorts and dinner with Luigi always made him feel better. It wasn't like he was cheating on Daniel after all; Luigi was married...to a girl. Meaghan had been really busy recently and they hardly seemed to see each other anymore. Oh they still texted incessantly, but it wasn't the same. Bain missed his best friend and he wanted to talk with someone who would understand.

"Hey Jude, is Luigi around?" he asked the maitre d. There was always a table for him so he didn't even have to ask about that even though the restaurant was packed.

"He's in the kitchen. I'll tell him you're here," Jude said as he led Bain to his table. "It seems we're really popular tonight," he continued in a voice which said he had some juicy gossip to impart.

"Do tell," Bain obliged. He wasn't above a bit of gossip now and then.

"Meaghan was here earlier today with some doctor guy. And then *Dean* came in after them and sat at another table, spying on them." Jude told him a look of utter glee on his face. "What do you think is going on?"

Bain was taken aback at this story, it did not sound like either Dean

or Meg. He kept his expression non-committal though. He didn't

want to fuel any gossip fires.

"Well I'm sure I don't know," he said.

"Oh," Jude said sounding disappointed. "Well I'll fetch Luigi."

Luigi didn't keep him waiting long, and when he did come, he was a

veritable mine of information.

Chapter 2

"Hey babe, we need to talk," Bain said as soon as Meaghan picked up. "In person," he emphasized.

"Yeah we do, I have some news!" Meaghan said sounding ever so pleased with herself.

"Good, well so do I. My place, one hour?" Bain asked.

"Okay. I'm heading out the door," Meaghan said.

Bain hung up and turned to Daniel who was curled up on the sofa next to him. "Darling, I'm gonna need some privacy for this conversation," he said to him.

Daniel made a face. "Wow, and here I thought we were past keeping secrets from each other."

"This isn't a secret. It's a private conversation. We can still have private conversations right?" Bain said.

Daniel had lasted longer than his average boyfriend. It was over six months now and they were still together, still going from strength to strength. Still, Bain wasn't ready to include him in his inner circle of trust. That would take a lot more than just having sex with him almost every night. I mean Daniel was fire; in bed and out of it. He also cooked like a dream – but Bain wasn't ready to say he knew him well enough to trust him with his friend's secrets. So he'd just have to take himself home right now.

Daniel sighed and stood up, "Okay then Bain. Have your private conversation. I'll just go home to my tiny lonely one bedroom apartment and pine away there for you."

That was another thing about Daniel; he had been dropping way too many hints about wanting to move in with Bain. They just weren't *there* yet.

Meaghan beat the buzzer by twenty minutes, "How did you get here so fast?" Bain asked.

"I took a taxi," Meaghan said breezing in and taking off her coat. "It sounded urgent."

Bain smiled, Meaghan always *could* read his tone and mood without need for words. He sighed internally. Luigi had been able to do that too…

"What's up?" she asked.

"Have you seen your boyfriend today?" he asked as a preamble.

Meaghan frowned in puzzlement. "Nope, the hospital had an emergency and I've been working all day."

"Is that *all* you've been doing?" Bain asked.

"Ye-es," Meaghan said puzzled by his tone. "I was at work all day and then one of my supervisors took me for coffee and then I went home."

Bain's forehead cleared and Meaghan's wrinkled even more to see it. "What's up Bain?"

"Well, did your…supervisor take you to coffee at *La Trattoria*?" he asked.

"Yeah! How did you know? Oh, Luigi told you?" Meaghan said, asking and answering her own question.

"Luigi told me that you were having coffee at his place and *Dean* was spying on you," Bain said sitting down on the sofa and crossing his legs.

"What!?!" Meaghan said.

"He thinks you're cheating on him?" Bain said picking up a magazine and pretending to leaf through it.

"Luigi?" Meaghan asked in puzzlement.

"*Dean,*" Bain said rolling his eyes.

"Dean what?" Meaghan said totally turned around by the conversation.

"Dean thinks you're cheating on him with your...supervisor guy," Bain said.

Meaghan stared at him as if she had lost the ability to understand English. "What?" she said at last.

"That's what I said," Bain said.

Meaghan ambled over and dropped on the couch next to Bain staring in front of her in shock. She took the whiskey Bain held out to her without a word and drained it.

"Why the fuck would he think that?" she said after several moments absorbing the news.

Bain shrugged, "You'd know that better than me wouldn't you?"

"Apparently I wouldn't," Meaghan replied dryly.

"So maybe you should ask him," Bain said with another shrug.

"Ask him why he thinks I'm cheating on him? He's never so much as brought up such a thing. Where would I even begin without ratting you and Luigi out?"

"Aww Meaghan, you're always so sweet and loyal. But I give you permission, throw Luigi under the bus."

"What? Why?" she asked.

"Because...the bastard broke my heart and I've never said a word about it. This is my pay back," Bain said.

Meaghan looked at him, really looked.

"Hey Bain?" she said softly. "How are you?"

"I'm good, how're you?" he replied automatically.

"No Bain. I mean, how *are* you?" she asked bending her head so she could meet his eyes as he looked down at the magazine.

He looked up and met her eyes and then he inclined his head in a gesture of helplessness.

"I don't *know*," he said leaning forward to rest his head against hers. "I *should* be happy. I *am* happy. But I feel so *restless*."

"You don't know what's wrong?" she asked stroking his thick brown hair slowly.

Bain sighed. "I think I'm just...I keep wanting things I can't have and not wanting the things I can have. It's stupid."

"What are you trying to self-sabotage this time Bain? Is it Daniel?" she asked.

"He could be a gold digger," Bain protested.

"Why coz he's a stripper? You've known that for six months. What's changed?"

Bain sighed, burying his face in her bosom. "Why can't I be straight? Then you and I could be together." He moaned. Meaghan smiled.

"Aww thank you Bain but to get back to the topic of why-" Meaghan persisted.

"You're such a good friend," Bain interrupted. "I mean you must be *freaking out* about Dean and the whole cheating thing yet here you are trying to sort me out."

Meaghan smiled, "Very good try Bain but you're not distracting me. What's up?"

Bain sighed again, "I think Daniel wants to move in with me."

Meaghan found that her mouth was open and closed it before the flies started moving in.

"Okay. And...?"

"*And*...?" Bain repeated in disbelief, "What do you mean, 'and'?"

"I mean, what's the problem? You two spend every night together anyway."

"That's different," Bain protested.

"How?" Meaghan wanted to know.

"I can always throw him out any time I like and we don't have to worry about who is paying which bill or how untidy he is."

"Okay so you don't want to permanently share your space with someone. Makes sense. Have you tried to tell him so?"

"I have…tried. But he has these puppy dog eyes…" Bain looked at her helplessly like he was at his wits' end.

"So what then? Break up with him, begin the search anew?" Meaghan waxed poetic.

"No. I don't want us to end. I just want us to go on the way we are now. Is that too much to ask?"

"You're asking the wrong person. You should be having this conversation with Daniel."

Bain smiled, "God I've missed you."

Meaghan lurched forward and enveloped him in her arms. "I've missed you too. Let's not disappear on each other again like this. Ever."

"Deal."

As if it had heard them, her notifications pinged. Meaghan looked at the screen expecting the hospital but it was a message from Dean.

I need to see you. Where are you?

It reminded Meaghan of the other message she'd gotten from Dean today, asking her where she was. She'd said she was at work, while she was really at *La Trattoria*. She glanced over at Bain who was still looking miserable wondering what to do. If she told Dean where she was he'd ask her to come over to his place. Bain and Dean

didn't live too far from each other. But she felt like she couldn't cut

short her night with Bain. They still had so much to talk about, catch

up with. He was her best friend long before Dean was her boyfriend

and she'd been putting him last for way too long. But...Dean

thought she was cheating on him. If it wasn't so sad it would be

really funny.

I'm at Bain's.

She typed and sent the message and then leaned back with a

second drink that Bain placed in her hands. She was just opening

her mouth to speak when her notifications pinged again.

Come over

He said, as predicted. Meaghan's head thunked on the seat rest as

she tried to think of a way to say no that wouldn't seem like

blowing him off...again.

Its girls' night Dean. Bain has some stuff he needs to sort out. He needs me. I'm off tomorrow though. See you then?

There. That sounded about right. She heaved a sigh and sent it with Bain looking over her shoulder.

"You can go if you want," he offered.

"I really can't. it's been a really long day; I don't think I can deal with tantrums tonight anyway."

Bain smiled. "Does Dean do tantrums?" he asked in amusement.

"Bain, if you'd asked me half an hour ago, I would have said Dean didn't do stalking. Shows how much *I* know."

Bain laughed, "Yeah. Wow, your problems are making my problems seem like made up or something."

"Nah Bain, I know you. I've seen you in pain. And you are in pain over something. Now we're going to get properly drunk and we're going to sort this out," she said in determination.

"Yes ma'am," Bain agreed with a grateful smile.

*****

Dean stared at the text from Meaghan, his blood literally boiling. He composed a text;

I don't believe that after everything we've been through you would-

Then he shook his head and erased it. He tried again.

How could you do this to me-

And then shook his head again vigorously grimacing with how pathetic it sounded and also how hurt he was feeling. It was pathetic and he never would have believed it of himself if it wasn't happening to him right now.

You lying bitch. Are you with him right now-

Dean almost sent that one but then he erased it because it sounded too much like the texts Samantha used to send him in the first months after their break up. He would not be that guy.

Never mind. It's fine. Whatever.

He stared at that one for a long time, thumb hovering over the send button. Then he hit it with a sigh and threw his phone on the bed. He stood up and extracted a full bottle of whiskey from the bar not bothering with a glass. He downed a good quarter of the bottle in one gulp and then lay down, feeling dizzy already. He had this heavy weight on his chest that he couldn't seem to shift and he just wanted to escape somewhere where he could forget. At least for a while. He leaned forward and snagged the whiskey bottle, cradling it like a baby. He moved back so that his back was against the headboard, and stared out his window at the stars of New York. They could possibly be lights, he'd heard it said that the stars over New York City were invisible. Either way, they were glowing pin pricks of light gleaming against a black back drop of infinite sky and he could get lost in it. Better than thinking about Meaghan maybe moving on from him, finding someone else...but why would she do that? They were happy. Weren't they? I mean the sex was off the charts regardless of Meaghan's relative inexperience. Dean could sincerely say he'd taught her everything she knew – and they'd discovered a few more things along the way too. They didn't have much time together, their schedules were crazy what with him running a company and she being an resident surgeon in training. It was a wonder they found any time to be together –and that doctor guy was at work with her all the time. They definitely could find more time to spend quality time together. Not that his and Meg's time wasn't quality. They'd certainly learned each other's bodies to an expert degree by now. But maybe they could possibly spend more time talking…she'd seemed so intensely engaged with the conversation she was having with that guy. They probably had more in common as well. Both doctors and shit…

Dean took a bigger sip of the whiskey and then another one for luck. By the time he blacked out, the bottle was three quarters empty.

*****

The pounding woke him up. He didn't know if it was in his head or from some external source. Either way he needed it to stop. He clutched his head, trying to keep it from rolling off the bed and onto the floor; possibly careering out the door and smashing into bits on the parking lot asphalt. On second thought, that would definitely stop the pounding forever so…

He squinched his eyes open and looked around. The bottle of whiskey was on the floor, bottle open and alcohol half poured on the woolen carpet. There was no way he was salvaging that. The carpet would have to go. Which was sad because it was one of his favorites – he'd acquired it at an antiques auction when he'd moved out of home. It was his first piece of furniture that he'd purchased for his new home. A home he'd envisaged maybe one day sharing with Meaghan...maybe more like fantasized. It wasn't like his family even knew he was with her. His father was still very much in the dark. And there was really no way to tell him without a guarantee that he wouldn't have a stroke. The thought of Meaghan made his heart sink; likely it wouldn't be a problem anymore now that she was moving on.

The pounding hadn't stopped and now his phone was ringing. Someone needed to make it all stop. He picked up his phone and answered it if only to stop it ringing.

"Make it stop," he whispered into the phone.

"Open the door Dean," Meaghan demanded.

"What?" Dean asked in confusion. He noticed that the pounding had stopped.

"Open. The. Door. Dean," Meaghan repeated biting off each word angrily.

Dean frowned; he didn't understand why Meaghan sounded so furious with him. He stood up slowly and shuffled to his front door; Mindy who ran the bookshop had opened up downstairs so at least he didn't have to negotiate the stairs; all he had to do was open the door to his apartment.

"Hi," he croaked as she stepped into his house and marched to the living room. "Please, come in," he mumbled as he closed the door and followed her slowly. He felt like an eighty year old man in the body of a two hundred year old man and walking was a real

challenge but he managed it.

Meaghan was standing the middle of his living room, arms crossed,

face like thunder.

"What?" he asked without preamble.

Meaghan's eyebrows went up and her lips twisted in that way that

said '*well excuuuse me*' without having to say a word. She fumbled

in her pockets with sharp angry movements and then her hand

emerged holding her phone. She brandished it toward him as if it

was a weapon, glaring at him the whole time.

"What?" he asked again, completely mystified.

She said nothing, lips pursed together, just shook the phone at him

like he'd ruined the battery or something. He reached forward

tentatively and took the phone from her, looking down at it at the

last minute after holding a staring match with her for a while. The phone was open to text messaging and he saw that she had

received a number of texts from someone...*him*.

How could you do this to me?

The first one said and he scrolled down reading the rest as he paled

even more than he thought he could.

I thought I could trust you.

WHERE THE HELL DO YOU GET OFF LYING TO ME YOU FUCKING

BITCH

Dean grimaced as he scrolled down wondering if he could possibly

make like this never happened.

Are you fucking him now? Is that what you're doing????

Slut

Dean switched off the phone after that message. He couldn't read

any more. He certainly had no memory of sending any of these. He risked a glance at Meaghan; she was breathing very heavily, eyes looking bloodshot as she glared at him. He opened his mouth and then closed it again completely at a loss as to what to say.

"What the fuck Dean?" Meaghan said and Dean exhaled the breath he didn't know he'd been holding. She sounded pissed but there was no hint of guilt in her tone. So maybe he'd got it all wrong and all the alcohol and misery had been for nothing.

"I'm an idiot?" he ventured.

"That goes without saying," she replied. Her self-righteous tone further lifted his spirits. If she was cheating on him wouldn't she sound more apologetic or guilty? Less like...she wanted to gut him like a fish?

"I...came by the hospital yesterday," he said slowly, eyes mostly on the ground as he darted occasional glances at her. "I wanted to cook you a nice dinner maybe, talk about your day. I heard about the accident on I-295; the news said most patients were taken to your clinic. I knew you'd have had a rough day." He glanced up and saw that Meaghan's expression had softened slightly. But her arms were still crossed and her stance was still combative.

"So then I arrive at the hospital and you're leaving with some guy who is entirely too solicitous of your welfare. And you take him to La Trattoria of all places and you guys are looking all cozy and intimate talking over your cappuccinos...it was...disconcerting," Dean continued, looking at her to see how she was taking all this. She was still listening intently but her arms were loosening up so that was good...he hoped.

"So yeah I followed you. But I texted you and asked you where you were and you lied to me. *You lied to me* Meaghan. What was I supposed to think? Furthermore, I ask you to come by and see me last night and you blow me off. What would *you* think?" Dean's voice had risen throughout this speech as he remembered his trials and tribulations of the day before.

"You couldn't wait to talk to me before you start throwing around accusations and insults?" Meaghan asked coldly.

"I was blind drunk Megs, I can't even remember sending those texts."

"Wow, you're blaming *drunk texting*?" she demanded.

"I'm not blaming it. I'm just telling you how it was," Dean clarified. "Now my head is pounding like a motherfucker and obviously I was wrong, so if you're here to break up with me do it quickly so I can go finish up killing myself."

Meaghan stared at him, incredulity in her eyes. He stared back at her waiting. Suddenly she burst out into loud laughter, bending over and clutching her stomach with the force of it.

"God this is soooo stupid," she said in between snorts. Dean smiled tentatively at her.

"Yeah?" he asked hopefully.

"Yeah," she replied nodding her head. She straightened up still hiccuping. "Tell you what, I'll let you get your rest or your suicide on, whatever, and we can pick this up when you're sober and...not hung-over."

Meaghan took a step toward the door but Dean's hand snaked out and closed around her wrist. "Wait. You're not going to explain yourself?"

Meaghan turned to face him, the glare back in full effect, "Tell you what, we'll chalk that one up to you being hung-over, still drunk and filled with bitterness. It's your last free pass though. Let go of my hand." She bit out every word and her face was thunderous. Dean slowly let go of her hand and stepped back. Clearly he wasn't getting any answers today. Or maybe ever, who knew with

Meaghan? She took the last two steps that brought her to the door

and walked out without another word. Dean waited, swaying on his

feet to hear her footsteps climbing back up the stairs and her

opening the door to say that she was just kidding – of course she

would explain and he should quit being such a baby about

everything. Then she'd maybe put her arms around him and kiss

him like she meant it. And he would kiss her back, whisper

apologies into her neck and endearments into her skin. He would

let her know just how much she meant to him so that she knew that

all those insults were just the product of a breaking heart; he hadn't

actually meant any of them…

He waited and waited, but she didn't come back.

Chapter 3

Meaghan didn't go home; she was too upset and she didn't want to tell her mother the whole story. So she went to Bain's house. She had a key – for emergencies- which she hadn't used before; not wanting to invade his privacy. But if ever there was an emergency, this was it. She needed a haven to think, go over everything in her mind and come to a logical conclusion. She unlocked the door and stepped in turning to close the door behind her and lock it again. When she turned back, she was astonished to see a man brandishing a knife at her. It took her a moment to recognize Daniel; as he was fully clothed with his hair tied back in a ponytail. He was still handsome as ever, but in a different way than when he was on display at his place of work. For one thing, he seemed bigger, more manly. The way he held the knife...Meaghan was quite sure he knew exactly how to use it.

"Er...hi?" she ventured tentatively. "I was just er, looking for Bain."

www.SaucyRomanceBooks.com/RomanceBooks

Daniel lowered the knife slowly looking a bit sheepish. "Well, as you can see, he's not here – and I'm not expecting him any time soon either. He went to Baltimore for a site meeting with some new investors he said. Probably be back in the morning."

"Oh yes, he did tell me he'd be out of town," Meaghan agreed. That was actually one of the reasons she'd chosen his house to go to ground at. Looked like that plan was a bust…it looked like Bain had decided to take the next step with Daniel after all.

"Would you like to visit with me anyway? Bain goes on about what a great listener you are. Would you mind if I bent your ear for a while? I've got food; and alcohol," Daniel coaxed. Meaghan smiled; it might actually be good to listen to someone else's problems for once rather than wallowing in her own shit.

"Sure I could eat," Meaghan said with a shrug coming in. obviously she wasn't going to get her time of introspection, but maybe dealing with someone else's issues could be just as effective as dealing with her own. Who knows, maybe Daniel might have some insights as to why Dean was acting like such a dick all of a sudden. And besides, if Daniel was going to be an important part of Bain's life, then they'd do well to get friendly-er.

"I've prepared meat loaf. Do you like meat loaf?" Daniel called walking back to the kitchen.

"Yeah sure why not?" Meaghan replied because not having tasted Daniel's cooking before she wasn't sure what she was in for exactly. The smells emanating from the kitchen though, were making her mouth water despite her misery so she has to conclude that he knew what he's about. She found Daniel leaning over the stove, a plate in his hand, serving something out of a pan and moved closer to see if it was the source of the smell; sure enough, there was a piece of meatloaf on the plate and it smelled damned good. Meaghan took the proffered plate and moved to the living room while Daniel followed with his own plate, and some wine glasses.

There was already a bottle of vino opened on the coffee table and Daniel put down the glasses on the table and poured some Cabernet Sauvignon into the glasses. Meaghan lifted her brow impressed at the vintage but also uncomfortable in drinking Bain's expensive wines when he wasn't there.

"Does Bain know you're raiding his wine cellar?" she asked, echoes of the conversation she'd had with Bain about Daniel being a gold digger at the fore front of her mind.

"Actually he's the one who opened this bottle to toast us earlier. I told him I'd polish it off as a consolation prize for not having him in my bed tonight."

"Aww," Meaghan said only half-mockingly.

Daniel smiled and shrugged, "Aaand we can neatly segue to how he's been pulling away from me and then he calls me this morning and he's all 'let's work things out'…I'm thrilled. I am. But I don't understand."

Meaghan tried to look as non-committal as possible and not like she'd been taking Daniel apart with Bain just last night and putting him back together. Bain hadn't told her what he intended to do after their all night therapy session in which they'd destroyed more than one bottle of expensive wine; but he had said that he felt more clarity than he'd had in a long time.

"So why didn't you tell him that?" she asked Daniel.

"I did; but we were out of time – he had to go or he'd miss his plane. I'm just asking you Meaghan, if you can fill in some blanks for me. Just a bit of quid pro quo. I'd owe you," he coaxed.

Meaghan studied him thoughtfully; this was a good time to really explore Daniel's motives. Meaghan was a fairly good judge of character, she thought. She knew Bain, knew that he was conflicted about relationships and being hurt and getting serious with someone who wasn't from the 'country club set'. As much as he lived his life parallel to theirs, he still craved their approval though he would never admit it. Even as he went out of his way to choose partners who would never meet with the approval of either his parents or his peers. Too outré for most of them; Meaghan knew she was a beneficiary of this twisted philosophy – she and Bain never would have gotten so close if he wasn't fighting this conflicting duality of his personality. He was attracted to Meaghan because she was an 'outcast' in their society. She was from the wrong side of the tracks and her ancestors certainly hadn't come over on the Mayflower. Still, whatever prompted Bain to befriend her, it wasn't the reason they were still friends and she knew that too. So now he was confronted with having real feelings for Daniel while being unsure of Daniel's social suitability to be his mate. He might be biased when speaking on Daniel's motives; stemming more from wishful thinking than reality. Wanting Daniel to be using him so he'd be justified in ditching him when they got too hot and heavy. So Meaghan could find out what lay on the other side of that equation. If Daniel was indeed here for what he could get that was one thing and Meaghan would be the first to kick his ass on Bain's behalf. On the other hand, if he had real genuine feelings for Bain then he needed to understand that any future he envisaged with Bain might not really come to fruition. Meaghan leaned back in the seat, body suddenly gone weak as she realized something.

'Is that how it is between Dean and me?'

Was he using this alleged indiscretion of hers to pull away from her. She remembered the birthday party his mother had held for him at the offices of Wesson Diamonds in which all the senior executives were invited and Samantha Crawford had stood beside him as if they were still a couple. His workmates had certainly treated her as such; and so had his mother. Dean had *said* he'd tried his best to extricate himself from the situation with minimal embarrassment to everyone concerned but Meaghan wasn't so sure now. Maybe he'd just played along with the whole farce because he knew that at the end of the day, Samantha was the 'right' one for him and not Meaghan. Maybe this was just-

Meaghan cut off the thought right there. She'd decided when she was embarking on this path that this was just a fulfillment of a teenage crush. It wasn't about marriage or a future...

"Meaghan?" Daniel broke her reverie, "Are you okay? You look a little pale."

Meaghan smiled, "Is that even possible for me?" she asked, half teasing.

Daniel shrugged. "Okay you look like you just swallowed an almond," he corrected.

"I'm fine. And we were speaking about you. Tell me, what exactly is it that you feel for Bain?" she asked.

Daniel seemed to take the question really seriously; thinking about it for a while before opening his mouth to say anything, "Bain is a really funny guy. He makes me laugh. And his heart...his heart is just really...open and pure," Daniel was rubbing at his chest as he talked about Bain's heart. "He cares about things. The other day I told him about my brother."

Daniel glanced at her uncertainly, as if he wanted to divulge something to her but it was personal.

"What about your brother?" Meaghan asked gently.

"He has HIV," Daniel said and grimaced at her. "I'm the gay one but he has HIV," he said wryly.

"That's too bad, is he on treatment?" she asked. HIV was something that Meaghan had come across a lot. She worked in an inner city clinic after all.

Daniel shrugged. "He has the drugs, and sometimes he even takes them..." he seemed sad and resigned. "Well anyway, I told Bain about him - we live together and he'd come home high after disappearing for a few days. I didn't know where he was and I knew he wasn't taking his meds because he left them at home – and he was just so concerned and he wanted to know how he could help...I mean, his life is great, perfect. He had no reason to even bother himself about my stupid brother and his stupid problems but he was there for me. I think...for real...that was the day I knew he was the one. You know?" he turned those dangerous gray eyes on Meaghan, looking so sincere and earnest that she knew she was lost. She wondered how Bain even had any room for doubts when he had those eyes looking at him like that all the time.

"Bain is great," she managed to croak out.

"He's...he's the most amazing human being ever," Daniel said smiling softly, eyes distantly thoughtful.

"Have you told him so?" she asked curious.

Daniel huffed a laugh. "Ha, like he'd let me. You know Bain, deflect deflect deflect," he said.

"Really?" Meaghan asked intrigued. Bain wasn't like that with her. They talked about their feelings all the time. Of course it was usually their feelings about other people they were discussing. Hmm, come to think of it – and Meaghan was surprised she hadn't before – her and Bain rarely talked about how they felt about each other. It was all just...taken for granted. Of course you could say that action spoke louder than words and in their case they were always there for each other, 100% of the time so maybe articulating feelings weren't necessary. It had never occurred to her that Bain might be uncomfortable with discussing emotion.

"But you know he cares right?" she asked Daniel.

Daniel shrugged. "I guess I do. He's an action guy you know; turns up for all my shows when he's in town, helps me out with whatever I need...he listens when I talk. It's not just about how long my legs are or how hot my hole is or how pretty I am," Daniel said smiling slightly, then his smile widened and he looked pleased. "Although he does tell me I'm pretty a lot."

"Yeah, Bain's great with compliments," Meaghan agreed affectionately.

"Not just that. But like at work, when those guys tell me I'm pretty, most of the time I just feel objectified. When Bain says it...I just feel appreciated," Daniel said looking into the middle distance with a thoughtful look on his face. "God, I miss him," he continued quietly.

Meaghan laughed, "He's been gone like...six hours?"

"Probably less. But talking about him like this, just makes me wanna…" Daniel trailed off and shot her a glance that let her know *everything* that Daniel wanted to do to Bain.

"I envy you guys," she said wistfully.

"Why? You have that hot Dean who's all over you all the time. Seriously that white dude has got it *bad*." He teased.

Meaghan laughed. "Really? You think so?"

"I *know* so" Daniel said very definitely, reaching out to rest a hand on her knee.

Meaghan was silent for a while. "He accused me of cheating on him today. Sent me some really nasty texts in the course of last night basically calling me everything from a slut to an evil cruel black-hearted gold digger," she said sadly.

"Wow. Why?" he asked, brow furrowing in confusion.

Meaghan shrugged, "I had coffee with a colleague." Daniel tilted his head curiously to the side like she was some exotic bird he was trying to make sense of.

"Just coffee?" he asked as if he suspected she wasn't telling him the whole story.

"Just coffee. He followed us to *La Trattoria* and watched us drink it. He might also have texted me at the time to find out where I was. I said I was at work; which I kind of considered I still was because this is my supervisor and he's kind of debriefing me about a tough situation that we had at the hospital."

"Did you tell Dean the whole story?"

"I shouldn't have to!" Meaghan protested. "This is a matter of trust."

Daniel was silent for a bit, looking like he was thinking hard. "I appreciate that Bain comes to all my shows. But I don't think he does it just to support me," he said at last.

Meaghan lifted her brow at him, her cure for him to continue.

"He's making sure that all I do *is* work," Daniel continued.

"You're saying he doesn't trust you," Meaghan intoned.

"I'm saying…he needs to know he can trust me so he's keeping watch."

"That kind of seems to be contradictory to me. If he trusts you, he wouldn't need to watch you."

"I guess it hasn't been long enough for him to feel like he can just leave me to my own devices in a roomful of men looking for sex, or sexual gratification and just be okay with that. I'm okay with him not being okay. He gives me enough space to work; but at the same time, he's possessive of me. I kind of like it."

"Well all due respect Daniel, there's no men at my work place looking for sexual gratification," Meaghan protests.

"Yeah, maybe. But there *are* men who are powerful and attractive who are known to date their female workmates. How many hospital shows are on TV? In all of them, the doctors are sleeping with each other, or with the nurses. Your shifts are long right? These people they spend more time with you than he possibly could...and now you're having coffee with one of them? Look at it from his perspective."

"So I'm not supposed to socialize with my workmates?" Meaghan asked incredulously.

"Socialize if you want; but don't lie about it. Expect your boyfriend to be insecure about it. If he wasn't, you should be worried. It would mean he doesn't care."

Meaghan sighed, thinking about all this. Relationships were so hard...who knew?

"So what should I do then?" she asked Daniel. Who would have guessed that he'd be such a mine of knowledge and wisdom?

"Exactly what you told me to do with Bain. Talk to him," he said.

Meaghan laughed softly, "I did kind of leave him high and dry."

"You don't want to do that. It just gives time for poisonous thoughts to fester," he said as if he'd been there, done that.

Meaghan fished into her bag, searching for her phone. She extracted it and saw it had gone off. The battery must have died; she'd neglected to charge it since last night, being rather distracted with other things. She sighed and plugged it in, sipping another glass of wine while they waited for it to get enough juice to switch on.

"Do you think Bain and I will make it?" Daniel asked suddenly.

Meaghan thought about Luigi and how that situation could only be labeled as 'it's complicated'. And then there was the fact that Daniel was a stripper and Bain couldn't exactly take him home to mama. Some people got into stripping as some form of rebellion but she had a feeling that Daniel wasn't one of them. Which meant that he couldn't just...stop. He'd need to find other employment and he had bills; stripping was probably more lucrative than any blue collar job Daniel could get and that was why he did it; she didn't get the impression that he enjoyed it. And if he was also looking after this sick brother of his, the hours were probably advantageous too. Like a cherry on top, he was as much from the wrong side of the tracks as Meaghan was. Worse than Meaghan because at least she was a professional.

On the other hand, Bain did spend a lot of time angsting about Daniel and worrying about whether or not he was using him. Which meant he was emotionally invested in this relationship. Would he have the courage to take Daniel on long term though? Meaghan couldn't say. Bain was one of the bravest people she knew but he chose his battles. Did Bain think that Daniel was worth fighting for? Did Dean think that Meaghan was worth fighting for? Meaghan didn't want to be drawing these parallels but they seemed to be doing it without any help from her. Daniel was right about one thing; she needed to talk to Dean.

*****

Her phone finally powered on to a series of notifications. It seemed she had a number of text messages; all from the same number. She sighed, wondering what Dean was going to tell her now. Maybe he was breaking up with her. Probably it was more insults. How many was one expected to take of those before the earrings, and all bets, were off? She scrolled through them, just to get the gist;

"I can't make you forgive me. I get that. I would if I could but I can't. But there is a choice, Megs, you know there is. I did a bad

thing, I get that. But you lied to me. You did a bad thing too. You know. But I won't… I won't make you forgive me. So you call me when you can, okay?"

That was the first message and it almost undid her. Meaghan didn't know how she was supposed to read through the other, God knew how many. She scrolled down, picking another at random. She'd go through them carefully later, when she was alone but for now she just wanted to see how bad things had got.

Please, Megs. Just. I need to know you're still breathing, okay? You don't have to call. And. And I won't pick up if you do. Just… something, okay? A text, just so I know you're… please."

Wow, Dean. Pleading. This was not a good situation they found themselves in. Things had gone left a bit too fast. She needed to get things back on track sooner rather than later. She scrolled down to the last messages.

"...you bitch, you fucking witch, why won't you just fucking... call me, Meaghan, come on, please. It won't be like a third degree or anything. I won't, okay? Not anymore, I swear I won't. I just want to hear your voice, please, Megs. Please-please, okay, just... fucking please."

Ouch.

She didn't know Dean even knew such language let alone spoke it. Her fingers skipped to the last message without reference to her brain. She had to know where his head was currently at.

I'm sorry. I'm drunk again. Seems I keep repeating my mistakes. You're turning me into someone I don't recognize Meaghan.

Meaghan's heart ran cold.

"Daniel. Thanks for the talk, and the wine and the meatloaf but I gotta go okay?" she said as she stuffed her phone and other things that had managed to creep out of her bag back in it.

www.SaucyRomanceBooks.com/RomanceBooks

"Sure darlin' I get it. Boyfriend shenanigans huh?"

"Boyfriend shenanigans," she agreed standing up. "Now I gotta go nip those poisonous thoughts in the bud before shit gets too real."

"Good luck," Daniel came over to her and enveloped her in his big strong arms. He smelled of sandalwood. Meaghan could not absolutely help that her heart sped up. "And thanks," he added quietly.

"You're so welcome. And thank *you*," she said disengaging herself from him. He smiled down at her with those devastating gray eyes. "I think you and Bain will be just fine," she said with a smile.

Chapter 4

Meaghan knocked tentatively at Dean's door, expecting that he would ignore her totally.

"Who is it?" his voice over the intercom was irritated and not exactly sober-sounding.

"Megs," she said voice trembling only slightly.

She was very surprised when Dean tore open the door and more or less tackled her into the opposite wall yelling about what an asshole she was. Meaghan's back thumped into the wall, breath leaving her like she'd been punched, because Dean was not really holding back. Meaghan's arms wrapped around Dean more or less in self-defense, because her body was reading this as an attack, and her heart rate was spiking accordingly.

She wasn't getting any kind of chance at recovery either or even getting a word in edgewise, because Dean's mouth was on her neck, talking wild and sounding angry, even if that's not what this was. Dean was just reacting, an over-abundance of adrenaline taking over him, more like. Jarringly honest and angry-pleased and calling Meaghan all kinds of things. Meaghan was completely bemused by this side of Dean. Perfectly capable of hugging the living hell out of her, while still hurling abuse roundly at her. It was so emotional and needy that it was kind of freaking her out. Meaghan just held on for a while. When Dean cursed low against her skin she knew this has gone on for long enough.

"Are we gonna do this in the hallway? Really?" Meaghan asked and Dean pulled back, smiling mad-glad and keeping one hand fisted in Meaghan's shirt so he could drag her along, even when Meaghan wasn't putting up any kind of fight and sort of laughing if only in shock.

Dean's surprisingly tiny apartment was not its usual neat and clean self. There was a bare brick wall at one end, which contrasted nicely with the yellow painted wall on the other, interspersed with bookshelves. The books were haphazardly arranged, almost as if someone had been riffling through them and not bothered to put them back in order. A few books were on the floor beneath the shelf as if they'd been dropped there by someone riffling through the shelves haphazardly enough to drop some books and not pick them up. Dean dragged her through the living room without pause, heading to his room. His usually neatly made bed was stripped, duvet trailing on the floor. Dark curtains on the windows blocked out the sunlight and the one small desk was overflowing with bottles of alcohol. A suspicious looking stain marred the beauty of the white fluffy carpet beneath the bed.

"Asshole," Dean said and grabbed on to her again and Meaghan was up against the door of the bedroom, Dean plastered to her front and … whoa, kissing.

Meaghan thought about putting the brakes on this, because wait, hold on, that's not... they needed to *talk*...sort things out. Well okay she'd expected he'd want to...but there's too much desperation and Meaghan didn't mean for this to be like that. Doesn't mean this to be like that. Meaghan got a hand on Dean's chest, feeling his heart beat trip hammering in his chest like he's ran a marathon or is scared shitless. *Is he scared shitless right now?* Fuck, Meaghan felt like she's in way over her head. She tried to push him away, to get her mouth free so she could ask but Dean made this sound, this low warning not-done-yet noise. Meaghan grabbed a handful of Dean's glossy dark soft hair and kissed him back just enough for him to lose some of the tension in his muscles and then she pushed him away none too gently. Dean's green eyes were dark, wild and half-closed when Meaghan got a peek at them. There was anger there, and fear; maybe something softer that she couldn't exactly name...

"Why did you shut me out like that?" Dean asked.

"I didn't know that I was. My phone died - know that sounds like a shitty asshole excuse but it also happens to be true – and I was trying to think, figure this whole thing out. Trying to understand why you would think that I would cheat on you."

Dean blanched. He really didn't like that, fighting to get back in closer, like that was going to prove some kind of point for him Meaghan was already getting an imprint of the door handle she was backed against into her skin and Dean was plastered to her front, so tight and snug. She was not all the way sure she wasn't going to have a bruise in the shape of Dean's belt buckle. Might get his buttons too.

"Chill out," she told Dean even though she *knew* it was a mistake. "No," Dean responded, perfectly reasonable, tone calm and sure, and pushed in closer.

Meaghan tried to squirm away from the door but Dean's grip on her was inexorable and all she managed to do was wedge him more firmly against her. From the way he gasped at her squirming and the hard length she could feel through her jeans, she guessed that this situation needed to be defused forthwith before they could hash things out verbally.

"You smell like wine. What have you been doing? Shit, I've missed you," Dean mumbled in between kissing licks at Meaghan's skin and then there was the rough slide of his hips, one hand coming up to Meaghan's neck and the other pressing to the ribs on Meaghan's left side.

"Peel me off the fucking wall and I'll tell you," Meaghan tried and Dean just huffed a quiet laugh, warm air skating Meaghan's mouth and then they're right back to kissing again, only this time Meaghan's not even trying to pretend to fight it.

She gave every bit as good as she got and Dean wasn't letting up. Meaghan started to feel like Dean was not going to be done until he had Meaghan like this right up against the goddamned door and it wasn't at all the way she'd seen this going.

"Okay, you know what?" Meaghan got out and pushed with her whole body, forcing Dean to take a step back unless he wanted to lose his balance.

Dean moved with her, still holding on to her, all easy compliance and soft stepping. Meaghan was too confused to even think about that until Dean's tongue rolled back into her mouth, slow and deep and with so much to it that she followed Dean without thought; not thinking about it at all, which was just so stupid, because Dean was so smart. And Dean was backing up so Meaghan had to step with him, keeping that golden roll going until they're at the bed and Dean was stripping her out of her jacket and no, wait, that wasn't the way this was supposed to go.

Because they do this. They try to sex their problems away and they don't talk and so far it's worked because they've been keeping things very much on the surface; trying to keep things easy and fun. And now Dean wanted things that Meaghan was quite sure weren't going to be appeased with a quick and dirty fuck, or even a slow burning meandering fuck. Dean's hands were all over her, though, so that when he pulled, she went down, landing half on top of Dean with her knees and elbows braced for impact.

Meaghan didn't have a prayer. She was truly, deeply screwed and it only got worse when Dean's hands found their way in under her shirt and Meaghan's legs spread for him without her conscious volition. They'd never done it like this before; in the middle of the knock down drag out they appeared to be having. He pressed his finger into her, seeking that nub of sensitivity that always turned her to soft blubbering mush when he rubbed it just right.

Meaghan tried to pull back, even with everything in her screaming at her to give in to it instead. Dean's fingers were buried deep within her working her like a guitar and he was still rolling his hips in that clever way that doesn't make things any easier. Meaghan didn't come here for this. Shit, she wasn't sure what the hell she thought she was coming here for. In hindsight she should have known. Truth be told, though, some things are what they are, solid and significant and not at all that easy to get around.

Dean was looking at her, light shining out of his eyes and a sharp edge to his smile.

"Are you going to make me ask? Beg? Really? 'Cause I will, I swear," Dean said and Meaghan wanted to jump in right away with reassurances that she would *never*...the look in his eyes; did he even know how he was looking at her right now?

Dean had a wide bed, suitable for playing any games they might imagine and there was scant light playing around in the gloom of the darkened room. And Meaghan was lost. She knew from the moment she left Bain's house to come here. She might have told herself that she wasn't coming for this but that was not exactly the truth. Whatever craziness might come between them, they would always have this. Maybe it was because Dean was her first – and she knew no other. She didn't know why, but every time she was in his vicinity, she felt the pull of this thing between them like sex was a drug and she was an addict. Meaghan propped herself on one elbow, chest pressed tight against Dean's, and ran her free hand up Dean's neck, over his jawbone, up his temple, light careful fingers combing slowly through Dean's hair, pushing it out of his face. She took in the flush, the hectic light in Dean's gaze, the shadows lurking there and the dark smudge under his eyes. Clearly this thing was taking its toll. Meaghan was sorry about that. She hadn't meant for this to happen.

"I didn't come here for this," Meaghan tries to say. "I wanted to clear things up with you," she continues but her voice goes deep and husky when Dean rolls his hips up again, thighs flexing and relaxing the better to strain against her and his hand so warm on Meaghan's back.

"I know," Dean says slowly, softly, like a promise. "I thought that was what we were doing."

And just like Meaghan had been thinking that's sort of the problem. There were things they couldn't sex away. And Meaghan was pretty sure distrust was one of them. They needed to develop better communication skills, and the only way she knew how to do that was by actually talking. She thought that she probably shouldn't be lying on the bed on top of her boyfriend – was it really boyfriend if no-one is supposed to know they're together? - thinking about how to make good on the promises in Dean's eyes, in his voice, made with his hands. Meaghan had really just come here to make sure that Dean was okay.

"Dean..." Meaghan tried again even though her brain felt lobotomized. Dean's hands were so far inside her, she was pretty sure he was brushing against her *womb*. Why was it not his penis again?

"No. You're here. That's. It's okay. It's just … you and me."

Meaghan wasn't sure that it was okay but she was willing to go along with it for now. They could always talk after, after all. Except that they never did. She's tried before. Dean always cuts her off before the conversation can really get going with a kiss, or a murmured 'it's okay'. And she's let it go before because it *was*… okay. At least she'd thought it was. But then Dean fell apart over nothing more than coffee with a colleague…clearly everything isn't fine. Still, they could postpone talking for another hour or so right? Dean was so warm under her, so close and so good.

"Be here with me, okay?" Dean whispered against her skin.

Meaghan figured this was what it was and lowered herself enough so that her lips could touch his; lost in the sweetness, like there was even a choice to make here. Dean was languid against her just long enough for Meaghan to get lulled by it and then his hands grasped and held on and he hooked a leg behind Meaghan's knee, sliding his mouth away to talk, hot against Meaghan's skin, about exactly what he wanted her to do to him, and Meaghan knew she was going to, even when she was still shaking her head.

Dean's words send heat skating down her spine and she shivered all the way through in a way that made Dean laugh low and content when he felt it. Dean was smart enough, always smart enough. He knew what to say and how to say it. The dirtiest words he could find turned into appeals and Dean was already moving against her, the deep driven need making that too good already. Meaghan wanted him so deep inside her that he couldn't find his way out again. She wanted to tell him but she was still shy. Dean didn't have any of those restrictions. Dean told her everything he wanted, every dirty detail, while he worked on Meaghan's clothes and his own. And no matter how Meaghan tried to tug and pull and shift them, Dean stayed on his back, keeping Meaghan pressed in close but nowhere near close enough for her. When Meaghan tried to slide down his body Dean held her right where she was, long legs and strong hands and talking, all the while talking like Meaghan was not going blind from all this already.

"No, no, no, not this time. This time you're fucking me, Meaghan. I want; I want you to fuck me. I've been taking the lead long enough, showing you the ropes. It's your turn now Megs. Show me a good time."

And, Christ, Dean didn't fight fair. Not that Meaghan exactly expected him to.

The way they were together on Dean's luxurious bed made the time between now and before seem inconsequential. It was all haze and dream shift, nothing noteworthy going on between here and there, despite the misunderstandings and the insulting texts, the drunkenness and uncertainty; not to mention the blood and gore and death Meaghan experienced just yesterday in a way that was too immediate not to scar her psyche; and she really needed to not be thinking about blood and gore when she was working her fingers steadily up and down Dean's penis while licking at his balls with her tongue and thinking about maybe putting a finger up his ass to see if that prostate thing was true.

It all blew straight out of her mind like so many dried autumn leaves when Dean reached down and slid his own long slender middle finger into her again mimicking the rhythm of her hands on him while making the dirtiest pleased noise Meaghan had ever heard in her life. She cursed at Dean and Dean groaned a laugh back at her.

"Taking too long," Dean ground out as he intensified his burrowing into her. There was a bit of pain mixed in with the pleasure at the force of it.

Meaghan wasn't arguing that. If the bastard wanted it so bad, Meaghan was going to give it to him. Meaghan meant this to be slow torture for Dean; just lay him out and take her time bringing him to a slow boil; but already Dean was shaking with it, hips shifting and a fine sheen of sweat breaking over the flush of his skin and Meaghan could feel that familiar force gathering from her center wanting to explode like a nuclear device and spread its noxious clouds all over her body; and she was already there, already in position before she thought it all the way through. Dean was moving into it, hips rising and Meaghan was done thinking about what should and shouldn't be by then, if she'd ever really paid it any serious mind.

There were things about this that hit harder than Meaghan expected. It wasn't the fact that he had heat running like a team of wild horses through her blood, or that she had a strangely known desperation bubbling under the rising pleasure. Those things were all about her... It was more got to do with how Dean searched out her eyes and kept coming back to her mouth, craning his neck up to be kissed over and over, shallow but sincere. It was breaking and mending things in Meaghan, all that need and desperation. He'd

ceded all control to her, she was in charge of how fast or how slow

they moved. She found that she wanted to grind down and swallow

him into her, his penis never to be seen again. The heat was already

spreading throughout her, weakening her, liquefying her limbs and

blurring her vision so she couldn't coordinate her body anymore.

Dean surged upward, lifting her clean off the bed as he strained into

her and then dropped them both down onto the bed. He gripped

her hip bones, so tight she knew there'd be bruises in the morning,

better there than her arms or her neck she figured – no need to

explain them at work – and lifted her up only to drop her hard onto

him again. She definitely felt that one deep inside and it made her

want more and more but her body couldn't take it and she was

shuddering and shaking as her orgasm was shaking her, causing

tremors to roil uncontrollably through her like an earthquake. The

sounds Dean was making would be embarrassing at any other time

but right now they just made the tremors worse. Her body arched as the feeling exploded through her, eyes wide and vision going white. Dean collapsed beneath her as his orgasm runs its course but hers seemed to go on and on, reignited by the slightest friction. Meaghan thought there was a possibility she might black out, maybe die...

She came to sometime later to find herself tucked cozily into Dean's blankets. She was naked under the quilt and every part of her ached like she'd done Zumba for five hours straight. She sat up in bed wondering where Dean got to and did she just black out from having sex and was that normal or did she need a check up? Maybe she's anemic?

Dean walked into the room in navy blue boxer looking like every girl's dream of a guy in boxers and Meaghan couldn't help smiling.

"Hey sexy," she said. Her voice was very hoarse; was she screaming? She couldn't remember screaming.

"Hey yourself," he said depositing the tray he was carrying on her lap. Meaghan watched him as he carefully positioned the stand so that it sat true. "Hungry?" he asked softly.

"I could eat," she shrugged.

Dean laughed softly and looked up to meet her eyes. They stared at each other intently.

"We need to talk," Meaghan said eventually.

"Yeah, we do," Dean agreed. His skin was flushed. It could be due to the lovemaking...if such a tame word could be used for what they did...but Meaghan didn't think it was. He was nervous.

"About feelings and shit," she continued like there'd been no break in her conversation.

"I know," he replied still arranging her tray to his satisfaction.

www.SaucyRomanceBooks.com/RomanceBooks

"And probably have the 'where is this going' talk, maybe even 'appropriate invectives to use while mad at each other' talk," Meaghan continued.

Dean laughed out loud. "I know," he repeated, "and I apologize. Those names were uncalled for and an inappropriate way to treat a lady especially one who is also my girlfriend."

"Oh, I get the 'gosh darn that sex was good so I'm happy now apology'. Great." Meaghan said mockingly. Dean had the grace to look abashed.

"Meaghan-" he began.

"No it's okay. I get it. Or rather Daniel explained it to me," Meaghan interrupted.

"What did he explain?" Dean wanted to know.

"Oh he explained how jealousy, insecurity and caring come together in a guy and manifest as assholery," she said.

"That's...vivid," Dean said.

"But true though," Meaghan clarified.

"Well considering my behavior the last couple of days, I can't exactly refute that. I did mean the apology though and not because of the mind blowing sex. Well...not *only* because of the mind blowing sex."

Meaghan laughed wryly, "Well at least you're honest."

Dean picked her hand up and kissed her reverently. "Do you forgive me?" he asked hand held in both of his.

"Of course I do. I'm an angel like that," she said.

"Thank you," Dean said seriously responding to her words, and not her tone. He took a deep breath and looked up at her, smiling.

"So, Megs, you said we need to talk," Dean said.

"I did indeed," Meaghan replied.

"So bring it Megs. Let's talk," Dean said handing her the cup of coffee he'd made.

Meaghan took it and sipped and then put the cup down, lifting her head to look Dean squarely in the eye. "Let's talk," she repeated.

Chapter 5

"First of all, how are you?" Meaghan asked as she sipped her coffee and ate her cookies.

"Me?" Dean asked in surprise. "I'm great."

"Oh really? You don't look so hot"

"Chee thanks," Dean grinned wryly.

"You know what I mean."

"I know what you mean. And I'm great. I wasn't. Three hours ago I was a wreck who was contemplating doing something stupid in retaliation for something I wasn't even sure was happening. But now I'm great."

"Why? What's changed?"

"You're here."

"And that's all it takes? To turn things around, my presence?" Meaghan asked. Her tone was flat yet curious; displaying no other emotion but that.

"Not really. I don't know how to explain," Dean sounded hesitant. "It's not that you're physically here. It's that you're *here* here."

Meaghan thought about that statement. "You mean like you feel like I'm with you body and soul?"

"Exactly"

"And you didn't feel that before or…?"

"I did but then this whole fiasco happened and you seemed to be pulling away from me."

"I had my first crisis situation. It was gruesome," Meaghan protested.

"And I wanted to share that with you. That's why I came to the hospital," Dean shot back.

Meaghan stared incredulously at him. "Really? Why didn't you say?"

"BECAUSE I HAVEN'T SEEN YOU SINCE!" Dean shouted and then stepped back like he didn't know where *that* had come from.

Meaghan stared at him in shock. "Okay," she said slowly. "Well anyway…"

Dean inhaled deeply, his flushed face fading to pale as he tried to calm down. "Well anyway, bygones right?"

"Yeah I guess," Meaghan agreed. "Next item on the agenda; where is this going?"

Dean was quiet not knowing what to say. "Meaghan," he began in that tone which said she knew he was a snake when she brought him home so why was she wanting to turn him into a teddy bear now?

"I just want to know what you want out of this thing that we're doing. I'm not trying to propose marriage here or anything," Meaghan clarified.

"I know that. Are you saying marriage is off the table then?" Dean asked, he just sounded curious, which kind of threw Meaghan.

"I'm saying it would be impractical to talk about marriage when you can't even introduce me to your father," Meaghan said.

Dean looked down, not knowing how to respond to that. "Okay, just for the record, I'd have loved to introduce you to my father. To my mother and my friends; have you by my side when we go to the symphony orchestra to be the guest of honor at benefits and soirées... I want you by my side always. And maybe one day we'll get there. But right now everything is about delicate balance."

"I know that. And I'm not asking for that to change. I just want to know, where is this going? Where do you want this to go?" Meaghan asked.

"I...think...I love you," Dean said sounding supremely uncertain.

"And what makes you think that?" Meaghan calmly asked as if she was a psychiatrist and he was on her bench.

Dean grinned at her. "I think the correct response is, 'I love you too.'"

"You mean, I...think...that I love you too," Meaghan said as if she was developmentally impaired.

Dean laughed. "I did not sound like that," he protested.

"Oh? I'm the one who had to listen to you so who's more reliable as a narrator?" she asked grinning back at him.

"We digress," he said.

"Yeah, we do. So are you going to answer my question or do you have some more deflections you'd like to get out of the way?"

"I think I can come up with a few more," Dean teased.

"Well bully for you. I'll just eat my cookies while you work through your issues. When you're through, you can let me know by answering my question."

Dean sighed. "I know that I...*probably* love you because the thought that I might lose you these last two days has been making me crazier than a dog in a hubcap factory. I tried to tell myself that my pride was hurt but I couldn't quite convince myself. And then you came...and everything was better and I knew I was fucked."

"And you were," Meaghan grinned.

Dean didn't respond to her joke. "I'm serious Megs," he said instead.

Meaghan stopped smiling, "Okay then."

"So…you ask a lot of questions but I don't see *you* giving much of yourself in this conversation. How do *you* feel about me and where do *you* want this to go from here?" Dean asked her.

"Hmm, you pose an interesting hypothetical?" Meaghan said.

"Why hypothetical?" Dean asked drawing away from her a little bit because he thought she was playing with him.

"Because whether or not I want something from this relationship – making it happen is not in my hands."

"You could at least be up front with whatever it is you want…" Dean coaxed.

Meaghan looked pensively at him. "Well when I agreed to go home with you that first time, I rationalized it by saying that you were my teenage crush that I should have had years ago. So it was like wish fulfillment. The relationship I *should* have had when I was seventeen. I thought that if I slept with you a few times, the shine would wear off and I'd be left with a bitter after taste; sort of like

'what the hell did I ever see in this guy?' But then...well, I'm sure

you know as well as I do that the shine did not wear off. At least not

for me-"

"For me neither," Dean interrupted making Meaghan smile.

"So anyway er, yeah that didn't happen the way I envisaged, so I

told myself we were just having fun. It wasn't too serious. Just two

people who enjoyed each others' company, hanging out."

Dean grimaced slightly at this explanation.

"But..."

"But..." Dean repeated.

"Yeah, so now I just need to re-evaluate, you know. Realistic

expectations and all that," she said.

"Realistic expectations..." Dean repeated.

"Is there an echo in here?" Meaghan asked trying to lighten the mood.

"I want us to work...in the long term I mean," Dean said.

Meaghan shrugged, "I want us to work too; but I don't want to be Icarus on this."

"I don't want to make you false promises either Meaghan. But I want you to know that I feel committed to us. I feel like...I need you to know that you are important to me. Very."

"You're important to me too. Very," Meaghan repeated.

Dean smiled, "I guess there really is an echo in here."

"I'm crazy about you if we're being honest," Meaghan said making the smile on Dean's face widen.

Dean reached forward to take her hand in his. Meaghan shook her head. "Okay enough with all the rom com ending dialogue. Let's move on to name calling norms in civilized society."

Dean laughed, "Shall we say that it's not okay to call each other any names?"

"I think that would be wise," Meaghan agreed.

"I apologize again for my shitty slimy uncouth behavior."

"All these five dollar words just to say sorry..." Meaghan said airily to dispel any remaining tension.

Dean reached into his pocket and extracted an actual five dollar bill passing it to her.

"What's this for?" she asked.

"I figured actions speak louder than words."

Meaghan barked a laugh but removed her purse from her bag anyway and made a show of keeping the five dollar bill in it. "Apology accepted," she said with satisfaction.

Dean smiled at her expression. "Look at that self-satisfied smile, who wouldn't fall for that?"

Meaghan shot him a glance and a smile but said nothing, just returned her purse to her bag.

"So I should get home. My mother hasn't seen me all week and my new fake boyfriend offered me a new job that I need to go research."

"What? Really? He was offering you a job? Why?" Dean perked up immediately looking wary.

"He grew up in Queens and he has a foundation which assists inner city youths in various ways. I expressed interest in it and he offered me paid employment so that would enable me to free up some time by quitting my locum and working for the foundation instead. It's a dream job for me to be honest."

"And he just happened to have it ready and waiting for you," Dean said strongly sarcastic.

"No. We talked about stuff and giving back to the community and he happened to mention that he has this project that he does."

"Y'all looked really cozy and all," Dean said the light of jealousy brightening in his eyes.

Meaghan sighed. "So we're back to snarky and jealous?"

Dean shrugged. "Well I'm sorry if I feel a little jealous that *my* girl is having coffee with random hot doctors in her favorite restaurant when she's never told *me* about these hopes and dreams that she has."

"So you're saying that having heart to hearts would be something you'd be interested in?" Meaghan asked unable to keep the amusement out of her voice.

Dean shrugged in contrived nonchalance. "That's what people in relationships do right?"

"I don't know. You're the one who was in a relationship for like fifteen years. You tell me," she said.

"You making fun of me?" Dean asked.

"Absolutely not," Meaghan said hand on heart. "I just...I don't know how to behave when you get all serious and shit."

"Why not? How long have we known each other Meaghan?" Dean asked looking intently at her.

Meaghan shrugged. "*Years,*" she said grinning.

www.SaucyRomanceBooks.com/RomanceBooks

Dean grinned back at her. "You know me right? I mean you know who I am right?"

"And you know who *I* am," Meaghan countered.

Dean shrugged. "I know who you *were*," he said thoughtfully. "Since we started sleeping together though…you're not as open as you used to be."

"I'm still the same basic person. Maybe a little more cautious but…" Meaghan protested.

"More cautious with me?" Dean clarified. "Why is that? Do you think I'm going to hurt you?"

Meaghan was silent for a while, staring down at Dean's duvet. "I know you will," she said quietly. "You might not want to; but you will. Because family always comes first. I know that about you at least. And I am not your family."

Dean opened his mouth to say something to that, protest maybe, but found that he had no counter-argument. Meaghan was right... but she was also wrong – saying so with his mouth though, would not convince her. She was a scientist – she liked empirical evidence that she could test out and touch and verify. Dean realized he hadn't really done anything to make Meaghan feel like she was just as important to him as anyone else in his life. Not really; he'd let his mother and Samantha manipulate him into a situation where the rest of the world was under the impression that he and Samantha were still together. His father thought he and Samantha were still together. In fact the only people who knew the true nature of his and Meaghan's relationship were Smith and his sister. Possibly the rest of his friends were aware that they were sleeping together or seeing each other; but they thought it was basically just one of those things...boys will be boys, sowing wild oats, whatever cliché it was this week. Meaghan wasn't a cliché; he'd said so to her. But not to anyone else. He couldn't really blame her then, if she thought that she really was just his flavor of the week or month.

"I don't blame you for thinking that," Dean told her now, his tone rueful. "It's my fault and I realize that now. I don't know what I can do to change it right away though. Any ideas?"

"Dean, I wasn't trying to make you-" Meaghan began to protest.

"I know you weren't," Dean interrupted. "I just...I'm out of ideas and I thought you might have some is all."

Meaghan smiled, leaned forward and laid a chaste kiss on his lips. She didn't want to give him any ideas – her body was still recovering from whatever that was they'd done just now.

"Let's just...put a pin in it for now. I think this is good. We've made some progress. We know that we have real feelings for each other. We know that it's mutual," Meaghan said with a shrug.

"I can't exactly stand up at the board of directors' meeting and say hey, you know what Samantha's not my girlfriend. It would be inappropriate," Dean said just thinking out loud, ignoring Meaghan's suggestion to put a pin in it. Meaghan huffed a laugh.

"Yeah where exactly on the agenda would that go? None of Your Business section maybe?" Meaghan said. "Look Dean, I get it. You're spirit is willing and so is your flesh. I didn't know before but I do now. You don't have to do anything, I promise."

Dean nodded his head, but he still looked skeptical. Meaghan pushed away the bed covers and slid out of bed, naked.

"I need a shower now though seriously, we'll get where we wanna go. Lets just not be all worried and shit. It'll come together by itself. I promise you."

Dean stood up and made as if to follow her to the shower. Meaghan put up her hand, palm outward.

"Halt. Where do you think *you're* going?" she asked.

Dean grinned. "I thought I'd scrub your back for you," he said hands on the waistband of his boxers.

"Uh huh. Not happening," Meaghan said eyes on his hands. "I still don't know how I'm even going to function after that...session. I'm not looking to inflict any more damage on this vessel," she said indicating her body.

"What damage? That was just standard sexual procedure for you; just coz you were on top this time doesn't mean anything changed," Dean said grinning smugly.

Meaghan threw a random sock at him and mock-glared. "Stay away from me fool," she said slipping into the bathroom and shutting the door.

"You don't know what you're missing!" he yelled at the closed door.

"Oh yes I do," she sang back as she switched on the shower.

www.SaucyRomanceBooks.com/RomanceBooks

*****

Meaghan and her mother walked into the narrow brick building that housed the offices of the Shelley project. She had an appointment with the project manager who would give her orientation on the work that they did here. When she'd told her mother about the work that Conrad had offered her. She'd been very excited and asked if she could come along and see what work they were doing as well. Meaghan had called Conrad to see if it would be alright and with his enthusiastic permission had brought her mother along on what was essentially sort of an interview.

"Hi," she said to the receptionist. "I'm here to see Maggie Martinez?"

The receptionist looked up, brown eyes friendly and welcoming in her freckled face. She smiled widely and stood up to point out the correct office; in spite of her substantial bulk and the gray in her hair she moved easily, guiding them to the right door and leaving them to it with a nod and a smile. Maggie Martinez also turned out to be enthusiastically friendly greeting Meaghan and Amanda like they were old friends.

"Conrad told me about you – we don't get many doctors who grew up around here so we're really excited to have you," she said as she led them down the hall to show them the clinic space.

"I'm excited to be here," Meaghan replied exchanging a look with her mom.

"Most of our patients are disadvantaged in terms of access to insured health care. We have a payment policy that allows them to settle their bills slowly at a rate that won't break them" she said as they walked past the packed waiting room where nurses were carrying out triage.

"And do you get many defaulters or are people good about paying?" Meaghan asked curiously.

Maggie shrugged. "Most of our patients are return customers. They are well known to us and we to them. I think Dr. Conrad told you that we don't just do the clinic, but we also have a mentorship program and needle exchange every other Saturday? We know most of these people by their first names; we've been to their homes. We know their challenges. It's a very hands on project we run here. Very few of our patients are walk-ins. And most of those who are have some sort of emergency or have heard of us through their neighbors for example."

As she talked, Maggie showed them the state of the art laboratory that had been built through the efforts of the community who held a funds drive to raise the capital. They also walked through the ward where a few inpatients were admitted.

"We don't have an extensive in-patient facility. Just a few beds to deal with acute cases that might need overnight observation. We also have a maternity ward though it's empty right now. Many of our maternity patients come from the drug users who are looking to give birth in conditions that are sanitary among people they can trust. Many times, they wish to give up the child."

"Sounds really intense. What do you do with the children who are given up? I mean obviously you call child services, silly question."

Maggie smiled, "Not silly at all; we have an arrangement with Child Services where we keep the child in the neonatal ward until we're sure that they are healthy. Many of them are born with addictions, and then we pass them on to the social worker who we liaise with."

"Maggie I'm really impressed with the work you guys are doing around here, even without seeing your other projects. So I just have one question for you," Meaghan said smiling.

"What's that?" Maggie asked head cocked, ready to answer anything.

"When do I start?"

Chapter 6

Dean was making more of an effort with Meaghan. She didn't really know how she felt about that. It felt a little forced. He'd text her randomly throughout her day giving her updates on what he was doing and asking what *she* was doing...it kind of felt like checking up on her. Who knew that beneath the expensive Armani suits and Ralph Lauren shirts beat the heart of a possessive jealous Neanderthal who thought he was being clever by couching his tabs-keeping behavior in terms of concerned and loving texts. She knew what his game was though she kept this knowledge to herself for now. No need to rock the boat unnecessarily. He also came to pick her up from work more often than not. So at least now everyone at work knew her boyfriend drove a flashy Lamborghini if not who he actually was. Thankfully her days were too busy for her to be pinned down by curious colleagues who wanted to know all about her guy. She was not about that gossip life.

She and Bain had kept their pact to not let busy lives get between them again. They had a standing Thursday night dinner date to which significant others were *not* invited, no matter how much they begged. And Daniel was not above begging...neither was Dean but he was more subtle about it.

*****

"I hear you're spending a lot of time in Queens these days," Smith ventured as they caught up at lunch; "citizens are concerned."

Dean looked up from his plate with a glare. "Concerned about what?"

Smith shrugged. "That you're...little diversion...is getting more serious by the day," he made air quotes with his hands around the little diversion.

"Yeah well it is getting serious; and it's not a 'little diversion'," Dean replied grumpily.

"Oh I know that, but the citizens don't. And that's why they're worried. They think you're breaking poor Samantha's heart."

"Poor Samantha my ass. Hasn't that chick found some new boy to toy with yet?" Dean's lip curled in annoyance and Smith laughed.

"You talk like her now, have you noticed?" he said.

"Talk like whom?" Dean asked getting whiplash at the twists and turns this conversation was taking.

"Meaghan, idiot," Smith said.

"Oh...no I hadn't noticed," Dean said and smiled.

Smith cocked his head to the side. "You look happier though," he said thoughtfully.

Dean's smile widened. "Man, you have no idea," he said spooning some rice into his mouth. Just then his phone rang and he glanced at it to see the caller ID. Normally he didn't answer while at a meal with someone unless it looked like a father-related emergency type call. This time though, his smile became a grin when he saw who was calling.

"Speak of the devil…do you mind if I answer?" he said.

Smith made a generous 'go ahead' gesture with his hand and Dean reached for his phone.

"Hi," he said.

"Hi," Meaghan replied. "I hope I'm not disturbing you?"

"No. I'm having lunch…with Smith. He says hi," Dean said.

"Hi Smith," Meaghan said but she sounded distracted.

"What's up?" Dean asked a frown marring his brow.

"Well I've just come out of a CME at the hospital," Meaghan began.

"CME?" Dean interrupted. "I don't know those words."

"Oh sorry, it means continuous medical education. Anyway we were discussing aids to facilitate people who are developmentally impaired," she said.

"Uh huh?" Dean said wondering where the hell this was going.

"There is some great technology out there," she said sounding a bit hesitant and Dean had no idea why.

"And?" he prompted. He was sure she must be going somewhere. It was in her tone, in the reluctance of it like she was afraid of his reaction. Was she moving away to study these things or something?

"Aand, well you told me how hard it is the fact that you can't communicate properly with your dad and I just thought that you might like to try this machine," she said getting the words out quickly and breathlessly like it would reduce the impact of what she was saying.

"I mean this stuff works; it basically takes brainwaves and transforms them into speech or movement. Yes it might sound a bit like terminator or whatever but many patients have benefited from its usage and at least your father would be able to articulate whatever he likes rather than relying on people around him to just guess."

"Meaghan, I need you to slow down and explain to me what you're getting at. No scratch that. When does your shift end?"

"Three o' clock. But then I have to be at the Shelley Project probably until seven maybe later."

"Okay then I'll come by there around seven and we can talk okay?"

"You don't have to I mean-" Meaghan began.

"I want to," Dean interrupted. "See you then."

He hung up and looked up to see Smith smiling at him.

"You. Have got it. Bad." he said.

*****

"The Brain Lab was one of the first to demonstrate that a person can control a robotic arm and a wheelchair with brain signals," Meaghan said as they walked through the clinic. It was Dean's first time at the Shelley project and Meaghan was giving the tour as she explained about her idea.

"It's possible to literally influence the wiring of the brain, rewiring the brain, so to speak, to allow them to make new neural connections, and hopefully to restore movement to a paralyzed arm." She continued looking at Dean to see if he understood what she was saying.

"It was developed to help people with various types of paralysis. Now your dad can't speak and this technology might help. Patients with locked-in syndrome consist of a smaller subset in need of such technologies. This is a rare neurological disorder where patients feel, think, and understand language, but cannot move or speak -- they are "prisoners in their own bodies, just like your dad," Meaghan explained.

Dean nodded his head to show that he understood. He was listening intently.

" For example you might have heard of Jean-Dominique Bauby, who became locked-in after a stroke, and wrote the memoir "The Diving Bell and the Butterfly" by blinking to indicate individual letters. Imagine that your dad might be able to move and communicate using the same technology." Meaghan said clutching at Dean's arm in her enthusiasm.

"There has been a lot of activity in brain-computer interfaces to help such people."

"So why haven't his doctors recommended it?" Dean wanted to know.

"It's all very new. It's actually at the pioneering stage right now. A research group laboratory for a guy named Miguel Nicolelis have shown that a rhesus monkey in North Carolina could, using only its brain, control the walking patterns of a robot in Japan. In 2011, they got a monkey to move a virtual arm and feel sensations from it! Can you imagine? The possibilities?" Meaghan enthused.

"And that's what you were learning about today?" Dean asked watching her face with affection.

"Yes," Meaghan replied beaming at him.

"So how does it work exactly?" Dean asked.

Meaghan explained to Dean that one technique that was used was to harness brain signals; known as functional near-infrared spectroscopy. The technique would involve shining a light into the brain to discern how much activity there is, and examining the corresponding oxygen level. Then light at a specific wavelength is beamed into the brain, and the oxygen present absorbs some of that light. This allows scientists to pick up on small differences in the blood's oxygenation. She gave the example of the Brocca's area which is a part of the brain that is crucial for language and is activated when a person talks inside their head or counts silently. The researchers had used oxygen levels linked to this to create a system that allowed the person to say yes or no just by thinking 'no'.

"So is all this technology available here?" Dean asked infected by her enthusiasm.

"The original hardware for a device that utilizes this technique was developed by Hitachi, and it allows a person with locked-in syndrome to say "yes" or "no," Meaghan replied. "But that's not all; the same people also developed technology that can help restore movement in people who have paralysis or partial paralysis in a limb. So your dad could be trained to use robotics to move his arm and maybe even his leg."

"It all seems too good to be true," Dean said in bemusement, a small smile appearing and disappearing on his lips like he was unaware of it.

"Yeah I know it is. But researchers really are looking at a rehabilitation robot called an exoskeleton, which is a device that a person sits in to be able to move limbs that they wouldn't otherwise. The robot can detect the brain signal corresponding to a person thinking about moving an arm, and then move the arm," Meaghan said.

"There is also a wheelchair that a person can drive by using brain signals, rather than moving a joystick or pressing buttons. Your dad would need to wear an EEG cap to measure brain signals, but setting one up is very complicated," Meaghan continued.

"Complicated but possible?" Dean asked hopefully.

"For you? I'm pretty sure it would be. Would you like me to make some inquiries for you?" she asked turning to face him as they came to the state of the art lab.

"I would be grateful beyond words," Dean said.

"Consider it done then," Meaghan replied.

Dean swooped down and kissed her thoroughly, uncaring of the people bustling around them in the corridor. Meaghan stiffened slightly but then let him have his way with her mouth. It was some big news.

"Thank you," he said softly as he let her lips go at last.

"Don't thank me just yet. We've yet to get answers."

"That's not why I'm thanking you," Dean said watching her with soft eyes and an affectionate smile.

"Oh? Why then?"

"Because you cared enough about a man you don't know to find out all this stuff that might improve his quality of life; just because he's my father."

Meaghan gave him a twisted smile. "S'no big deal," she said quietly.

"Oh trust me Meaghan, to me, it is."

*****

"I have some news for you," Meaghan said calling Dean early in the morning as she left for work.

"Good morning to you too. And how did you sleep last night?" Dean replied.

"Great, now you wanna hear my news or not?"

"Wanna," Dean said.

"I got you an appointment to talk with some people about that technology we discussed the other day. They would be interested to work with you on this; kind of see how well the technology does 'in the wild' as they say."

"Really? That was fast. I expected that it would take a lot longer to convince anyone to speak to us."

"Nah, they're really interested in trying out their technology. It's just that it's a huge and expensive undertaking that medical insurance really isn't willing to pay for."

"And we don't have that problem right?" Dean said wryly.

Meaghan shrugged although he couldn't see her. "The perks of being a millionaire."

"Excuse me, that's billionaire my girl," he said.

"Whatever man. So you'll tell your father?" she asked.

"Actually, I was thinking that maybe *you* should tell him."

"Excuse me, what?" Meaghan asked wondering when Dean had gone off his meds.

"You should tell him; it was your idea after all and it's about time you two met anyway."

Meaghan was silent for a good long while.

"Megs? You still there?" Dean asked.

"Dean, I didn't do this as some kind of play to-" Meaghan began.

"Of course I know that – idiot," Dean interrupted. "I've been thinking about it for a while. This just seems like an opportunity too good to pass up."

Meaghan sighed. "Nothing has really changed Dean. Your dad is still ill and your company still needs the stability of right perception."

"Yes well luckily for me, I'm a guy so having a woman at my side is not totally crucial to my being taken seriously. And I think I've built up enough of a reputation in the past nine months to be perceived as fairly level headed and intelligent."

"Having the 'wrong woman' at your side could change that perception."

"Look Meaghan, I'm not saying we put out a full page ad in the paper announcing our engagement although frankly I don't see what's so wrong with being with a future surgeon general...I'm just saying meet my father. Let him know your name and that you exist and that his son loves you."

Meaghan sighed in trepidation. "Are you sure?"

"I've *been* sure. I've just been wondering *how* to do this in a way that no-one suffers any heart attacks."

"Okay then, when?" Meaghan asked.

"Have dinner with me and we'll strategize," Dean said.

"I can't tonight, its Thursday," Meaghan protested.

"Oh Megggsss! Can't you postpone just this once?" Dean complained.

Meaghan smiled. "No I really can't. We can do dinner tomorrow. Breakfast too if you want, I'm free this Saturday."

Dean huffed in contrived annoyance. "Fine. If it's all I can get. Tell Bain I hate him."

Meaghan laughed. "Hey you know you and Daniel could set up a play date for tonight...you're both such sulky bitches."

"Don't tease me," Dean said.

"I'm not, pinky swear," Meaghan replied still laughing.

"Yes you are and I will get you for it," Dean threatened.

"I look forward to it," Meaghan said as she came to the train station. "I gotta go; talk to you later."

"Yeah okay. Have a good day my sweet."

"You too honey bunch," Meaghan replied and hung up.

She was still smiling when she got to the hospital where a string of emergencies sucked up her day and spit it out mangled and chewed up. Two gunshot wounds, one, a child not more than eight years old; a case of domestic violence where the woman's septum had been crushed when her husband almost strangled her to death, her infant daughter screaming and crying continuously as they took her mother away to surgery. Child services had to be called because there was no-one to take care of her; three cases of broken bones from a particularly aggressive high school rugby game...it was one thing after another. By the time she fell into the seat opposite Bain at *La Trattoria* her brain felt fried.

"Bad day huh?" Bain said sympathetically as he handed her a full glass of wine.

"The worst," Meaghan replied draining it. Bain would get her home even if she got drunk so she wasn't worried. Bain was ready with the bottle as she put her glass back down.

"Tell daddy all about it," Bain said soothingly as he filled up her glass again.

"Shall we start with the woman who was almost strangled by her husband and her daughter had nowhere to go when the police came and arrested said husband and brought the woman to the hospital? The daughter was dragged away kicking and screaming by social services probably never to be seen again. The mother will never speak again in her life." Meaghan said sadly.

"Ouch. I don't know why you got into medicine Megs. The worst thing that happened at the construction site today was that two workers were rough-housing, one guy fell through the floor and maybe sprained his ankle."

"Yeah but you have to go to work wearing a hard hat coz a building might fall on your head," Meaghan countered.

"Maybe, but most of the time I'm in my air conditioned office drawing plans or meeting with clients. The hard hat is the only excitement I see in my life," Bain said.

"That, and going to Daniel's shows huh?" Meaghan reminded him.

"I don't know, I think I'm all strippered out, you know. Getting old. It's not half as exciting as it used to be. I just do it for Danny now... mainly."

"Really? You don't enjoy the ripped undulating bodies anymore?" Meaghan teased.

"Well..." Bain hedged and then they both laughed. They would talk about the harder things; later during desert; when they'd ingested enough wine to be free of what little inhibitions they had left. The tears, if there were any to be shed, would come later, back at Bain's place. Tomorrow they'd wake up and go back to their lives relieved and refreshed.

Desert was tiramisu and coffee spiked with alcohol and Meaghan was pleasantly buzzed.

"So Dean wants to introduce me to his father," she dropped the bomb casually, making Bain sit up and open his mouth, for once, at a loss for words.

"That is huge," he said at last.

"Don't I know it," Meaghan replied. "Thoughts? Advice?" she asked looking desperately at him.

"Be yourself. He'll love you," Bain said at once.

"Very helpful Bain," she complained.

"Yeah, I know it is. That's what I'm here for," Bain swayed gently in his seat. He was a bit more than buzzed. His driver was waiting outside though so no biggie.

"What about you Bain? Are you taking Daniel home to meet the folks? You've certainly been together like donkey's years now," she said teasingly.

Bain's face fell and he looked troubled and Meaghan's brow furrowed in concern.

"What is it Bain?" she asked.

Bain just shook his head. "It's nothing, I'm just...I guess I'm in Dean's boat right now; wondering how to go forward without losing the people I love."

"The people you love," Meaghan repeated softly. "And is Daniel one of those?"

"I think he is," Bain said with a sidelong smile.

"Yay, Bain is in love," Meaghan sang.

"Oh shut up," Bain said but with good natured affection. "Shall we move this party to my place?"

"Yeah. Let's," Meaghan said standing up. "Lemme just visit the lil girls' room, I'll be right with you." Meaghan took off with her bag to freshen herself and Bain lifted his hand for the waiter so he could settle the bill. He looked up and was surprised to see Luigi looking down at him. The look in his eye was...strange.

"Forgive me," he said.

"For what?" Bain asked.

"Eavesdropping," Luigi said staring Bain straight in the eye.

"Why?" Bain asked.

"Why what?" Luigi asked.

"Why were you eavesdropping?" Bain asked impatiently.

Luigi sighed. "I do that sometimes. It's the only way I can seem to get any information out of you. When you're talking to Meaghan. Do you talk to anyone else so openly?" he sounded wistful.

Bain stared at him. "I don't know what you mean," he said coldly.

"No. I guess you would not," Luigi said looking sad about it.

"Why do you care anyway, aren't you married?...to a girl?" Bain said, in a rather hostile tone.

"Because I am a fool," Luigi said casting rueful glances at Bain. "And you come to my restaurant every Thursday with your best friend and you talk about your love lives and I thought it was because you wanted me to know. So I eavesdrop. But you are in love with someone else now..."

Bain glared at him. "I come here because I enjoy the food and not the MARRIED chef who left me for a woman. I thought we were all being civilized adults about this."

"We were," Luigi said taking Meaghan's seat. "We are. But my stupid Italian feelings can't seem to disengage from you. What is a guy to do?"

Bain shrugged. "I think that falls into the category of 'no longer my problem'," he said.

Luigi nodded sadly, "Will you come back?"

Bain just shrugged and Luigi sighed.

"Tell this Daniel fellow he is an extremely lucky guy," he said standing up.

"I believe he knows," Bain replied his tone cold.

Luigi smiled at him and walked away, signaling to a waiter as he went to go over to Bain to settle the bill. Bain made sure to leave a large tip and just as he was finished with his transactions Meaghan came up and they left.

www.SaucyRomanceBooks.com/RomanceBooks

*****

Dean was waiting in the visitors' parking as she finished her shift. She thought that she really needed to think about getting a car to make her commute easier, though public transport tended to be much faster in New York City. Still, it'd mean that Dean didn't feel obliged to drive all the way across town to pick her up. She couldn't seem to make him stop any other way.

"Hi," she said as she slid into the Lamborghini.

"Hey yourself," he replied leaning toward her for a kiss. She planted a fat one on his lips and he made a noise of satisfaction as if he'd tasted a particularly succulent slice of pizza. This impression was enhanced by the fact that his eyes were closed.

"Should we pass by your place and get a change of clothes?" he asked.

"Nah. I already have some," Meaghan replied. Dean smiled.

"What you need I think is your own closet space at my place."

"Oh oh," Meaghan said leaning back on the seat rest and closing her eyes.

"What?" Dean asked grinning at her.

"You know it's serious when it's you suggesting I get closet space in your apartment. I've read in all the magazines that it's the girl supposed to push for that," Meaghan teased.

"Well aren't you the lucky one then," Dean countered.

"I guess I am. Do I get to leave my toothbrush too?"

Dean turned to her with a concerned look. "What do you mean? Don't you already have a toothbrush at my place? Or have you been using mine you skank?"

Meaghan laughed. "I have actually been using your spare one if you must know. Hopefully no-one else is as well, ugh," she said making a moue of distaste.

"Hey you're at my place all the time these days, you seen evidence of anyone else?" he asked.

"Nope," Meaghan conceded dryly.

"Well there you are then," Dean said. He put out his hand to cover hers in the seat and they drove in silence for a while. Suddenly he turned to her and said, "You're the only one for me."

*****

Carmen, Dean's housekeeper/cook had outdone herself with the food. She'd made a Mexican mix of mole, tacos al pastor and guacamole. The food was simmering gently on Dean's warmer, just waiting to be served up and Meaghan's mouth was already watering despite the slight hangover she was still sporting from last night. Dean poured her a huge glass of water first with a cucumber in it and she drank it down while he served up the food.

"Dinner is served," he said.

"Thank you," Meaghan said taking her plate and going to curl herself in front of the big screen TV, putting in the movie. They had been going through the Fast and Furious series in preparation to watching the last one and they were currently on Fast Five. She hit the 'play' button and leaned back, tucking into her food. Dean came to curl himself next to her and they watched the adrenaline filled opening scene as they cleared their plates.

"You know, before you I never used to eat in front of the TV. It was always on the dining table, which was always properly laid," he said.

"Oh, lucky table," Meaghan joked.

Dean nudged hard with his elbow, giving her an appreciative smile nevertheless. "Well anyway I was saying, the whole eating food in front of the tube is a new experience for me and I'm still trying to decide if it's good or bad."

"Well, it saves time. I mean I assume it's not only the table that wants to be properly laid tonight right? And we've been wanting to watch this one for a while."

Dean laughed and laughed, "God you have the smartest fastest mouth of anyone I've ever known."

"Er, thanks?" Meaghan said her cheek dimpling as she grinned at him.

"I fall in love with you more and more every day," Dean said quietly serious.

"Aaaahhh! And there you go spoiling the mood", Meaghan joked throwing her hands up in the air and nearly dislodging her plate from where she'd placed it on the coffee table.

Dean laughed again going back to paying attention to his food and the screen. Halfway through the movie he asked if she was up to drinking some wine but she opted for hot chocolate instead which he went to make promptly.

"Thank you!" she called after him. "You're the best boyfriend ever."

"Aah," he returned, "there you go killing the mood."

Meaghan cackled but then settled back to concentrate on the movie.

There was dessert as well in the form of chocolate chip cookies which went very well with the hot chocolate.

"You know it's a good thing I'm running around all day because between you and Bain you'd turn me into a fat lump of lard in no time with your feeding skills."

"If you dropped Bain like right now, you'd only have to deal with one person over-feeding you," Dean shot back immediately.

"Funny. That's exactly what he said about you! Great minds and all that I guess," she teased grinning at him.

He smiled at her, staring at her dimple as if it contained the secrets to the universe and then he stopped smiling but continued to stare; the look becoming more and more intense by the moment.

"What?" she asked with no sound to her voice and the pulse in her throat going a mile a minute.

"Come to bed," he whispered back holding out his hand to her.

"Okay," she replied taking it.

Chapter 7

Dean led Meaghan to his bedroom, walking her as if she was a princess on her wedding day. He placed her carefully on his bed and then picked up his remote. The sounds of Marvin Gaye permeated every corner of the room. Dean had excellent surround sound speakers and he knew how to use them.

"Hmm seduction surrender," Meaghan said smiling.

"We do have C&C music factory if you would prefer it," Dean said smiling.

"Huh, I'm more of an AC/DC girl myself," Meaghan reminded him.

"Okay then, how about this?" Dean clicked a few buttons on his remote and the sounds of Bon Jovi's 'Bed of Roses' swelled through the speakers.

"That's perfect," Meaghan said her smile widening in delight. "I've always wanted to make love to this song."

Dean bowed his head. "Your wishes are mine to make come true."

Meaghan had absolutely no come back to that so she stood up from the bed and unbuttoned her jeans instead. Dean watched her; his face going slack and his eyes darkening with desire. He didn't move from where he was, he just stood there and stared like he'd lost the ability to move his limbs. Meaghan slowly unbuttoned her jeans, pausing between each button to caress her flesh, making appreciative noises at the feel of her own skin on her hands. She could see Dean's chest rising and falling faster and faster and it gave her courage to experiment some more. Her hands moved up leaving her jeans half unbuttoned to push her shirt slowly out of the way as she caressed her stomach contemplating her navel with absorbed interest; like she was alone in the room. She pushed her shirt out of the way so she could squeeze her breasts through her bra and Dean made a sound like he was strangling. Meaghan ignored him and ran her finger round her nipple watching it harden to a point before she pushed the bra out of the way to grasp her

naked flesh. Dean was moaning from where he stood but he still

hadn't moved. She got her shirt off in one fell swoop, dropping it on

the floor and then rubbing at her breasts through the silky lace of

her bra. Dean took a slow dragging step toward her like he was a

zombie. He was making sounds like one of those things on the

Walking Dead too. Meaghan ignored him. She'd had no idea how

much fun being a tease was. Her hands moved back down to her

jeans, and unbuttoned them down to the last button. Then she

glanced up at Dean beneath her lashes as her hand snaked into her

jeans and she touched herself slowly. He groaned out loud and took

another step closer. Meaghan moved back and tripped over the

bed, going over onto her back, her hand still buried inside her body.

She went with it, putting her feet up on the bed and spreading

them slightly, rubbing at herself with increasing motion, driving

herself over the edge.

"Meaghan," Dean said voice so hoarse it could be he had pharyngitis.

She continued to stimulate herself, eyes closed, making noises of pleasure and watching Dean beneath her lashes. His jeans were tenting in such a way as to let her know that she had his full attention. There was a bit of a leak too, pre-come she guessed, staining the top of his jeans. He made no move to touch himself or release his erection. Just stared at her as her back arched and she shuddered herself to completion. All he did was growl deep in his throat like a wolf.

Meaghan sat up legs apart, buttons open but jeans still on.

"You liked that," she said, not asking.

"I loved it," Dean whispered and took a step toward her.

"How about you give me a show too? Fair's fair," Meaghan said.

Dean's eyebrows went up, "You want me to...?" He looked down at his erection in shock and she followed his eyes.

"Yeah," she murmured looking back into his eyes. He stared at her in surprise, trying to gauge how serious she was being. Then his hands went down and he unbuttoned his fly, letting his pants fall to the ground. He stepped out of them, took his erection in his hand and caressed it thoughtfully. She watched his every move, not even seeming to blink. Her hands ran up and down her thighs, caressing herself through her jeans like she was aroused again. Dean's erection jumped in his hands and he squeezed the bottom tight to stop himself from coming on the spot. Meaghan's mouth opened and her eyes narrowed as she made a small sound and he clutched himself, running his hand up and down his erection his hips undulating unconsciously; thrusting into the air.

"Meaghan," he whispered.

"Dean," she said right back in the same tone.

www.SaucyRomanceBooks.com/RomanceBooks

His hand was moving faster and faster. He took it up to his mouth and spat on it and then put his hand back on the tip of his penis and ran it down to the base, a slow long motion that had them both moaning in synchronized biting pleasure. It didn't take long before long ropes of milky substance were flying across the room and landing everywhere.

"Oh my God that was hot," Meaghan whispered taking a deep breath.

Dean walked toward her, coming to a stop above her and staring down at her.

"Take your jeans off now," he ordered and she hastened to obey, kicking them away from her as her eyes held Dean, or he held her gaze. It was hard to tell through the haze of desire she was floating in. He bent forward, still maintaining eye contact gaze shifting from her eyes to her mouth. Her mouth softened inviting him in and he bent forward taking her mouth as if it was food and he was starving. The kissing went on for a long time, with both of their initial lust sated they could take the time to savor just this; holding each other, sharing air and saliva – tasting and biting; enjoying the sensations of loving and touching without sexual gratification.

Soon though, the kissing took on a more desperate texture and the touching became more passionate, more frantic.

"Dean," Meaghan pleaded legs going around his waist and her hips thrusting upward, asking without words.

Dean's hands on her thighs were strong, pressing down into her flesh with no thought to whether or not he was hurting her. He was too far gone; not that she was complaining. He spread her legs wider and thrust into her, pressing slowly into her until she was sobbing with need.

"*Dean please,*" she cried eyes scrunched closed and breathing through her mouth in great big bellows of want.

"Please what baby? Tell me," he growled hoarsely into her ear as his hips went in and out of her like pistons.

"Fuck me harder," she whispered, blown away by her own daring. She could hardly believe she'd said that.

It was a red flag to a bull; whatever tenuous control he'd been holding on to broke. He was a wild animal pistoning into her and then swiveling his hips to get even deeper. Meaghan suspected she was going to have bruises on her intestines in the morning. Still, she wanted him to go faster. Harder. More and more; it could never be enough.

"Love you so much," she murmured into his neck as he pressed her down into the mattress.

He froze for a second and met her eyes with his. "I love you too," he said and then put his head into her neck and fucked her harder yet. Meaghan could feel the wave coming to overwhelm her, building up in her body until she had to let it go before it drowned her. She arched backward, letting it all go as wave after wave of emotion trembled through her making her whole body shake. She heard Dean give a shout as her orgasm triggered his own and the feel of his seed spilling into her made her shudder all the harder. She wondered if she was going to black out again. She didn't though, but her whole body was weak and drained. She turned the side, tucked her hand inside the pillow and closed her eyes, falling asleep right away.

"Good morning babe," a voice woke her the next morning and she struggled to open her eyes.

"What time is it?" she groaned.

"Nine in the morning. Dad is expecting us before noon so you need to get your lazy ass up."

Meaghan sat up startled. "He's expecting us!?!" she repeated.

www.SaucyRomanceBooks.com/RomanceBooks

"Yeah," he said.

"Why?" she complained.

Dean put the coffee cup he was carrying down on the bedside table and turned to face her, "Have you already forgotten all about your T-1000 thing that you were going to tell him about?"

"Well yeah…I mean no of course I haven't forgotten but I didn't expect that it would be this soon. I don't have anything to wear," she wailed.

Dean laughed. "What's wrong with your jeans?"

Meaghan flopped back on the bed and shook her head. "You don't understand anything do you?" she said in despair.

"We can pass through DVF and pick something up if you want," he suggested.

"I can't afford Diane von Furstenberg!" Meaghan laughed.

"I can," Dean said.

"Well thanks but-" Meaghan began.

"Are you or are you not my girlfriend?" Dean interrupted.

Meaghan stared apprehensively at him as if she suspected a trick. "I guess I am."

"Good, well if you read the fine print of your girlfriend contract it stipulates that I may buy you clothes for special occasions, not so special occasions or just a whim as I please," Dean said.

"Really?" Meaghan asked.

"Really," Dean confirmed.

"Well...the woman is always the last to know," she said ruefully.

"So hurry up and have your breakfast so we can go shop before your big meet!" Dean said clapping his hands like a track coach and exiting the room to go put some breakfast together.

Meaghan rose slowly shaking her head and went to shower.

*****

They did stop off at DVF and Dean made her choose the dress she liked without allowing her to even peek at the price tag. It was too comfortable, too easy to let him just take over and pay for her clothes. Meaghan didn't want to get used to this. It was way too domestic and spoke of long days and longer nights...together... forever. Meaghan shied away from that thought, not wanting to let herself even think about such things.

They drove to Dean's parents house...did she say house? She meant hotel. It was that huge and as far as she knew there were only two residents living in it right now. Of course there were also probably like a zillion maids and butlers too. She took a deep breath and took Dean's hand. All the years she'd known him and this was the first time she was visiting the home where he grew up. It brought home all the differences between them. The trailer where she grew up could probably fit snugly in the foyer of this house, with space left over. Meaghan found that her palms were sweaty and she was breathing really fast.

"Just relax," Dean murmured to her. Easy for him to say, it wasn't him on the chopping block here. He took her hand in his and led her up the stairs. The door was opened by a butler dressed in a tuxedo and Meaghan knew she was completely and utterly lost. He led the way up to Dean's father's room and Meaghan cursed the fact that she'd forgotten to bring notes. Bad enough meeting him as Dean's girlfriend but she didn't also want to seem like an incompetent doctor. Dean told her to wait while he explained the situation to his father.

"I won't be long," he murmured as he went into the room. Meaghan crossed her arms and waited, trying to slow her rapidly beating heart. Dean hadn't lied, he was not long and soon he was leading her in to a room that looked familiar because it was set up like a hospital room. The man on the bed was hooked to various machines, a heart monitor, dialysis machine...yet she could see that effort had been made to brighten the room. The bed was facing a wall of windows which let the sunshine in and provided an unhampered view of the entire garden. There was a basket of fruit artfully arranged on the bedside next to him and the shelf by the wall was lined with flower arrangements probably sent by people paying their respects to the man in the bed. He had Dean's eyes... and they were studying her intently like if he looked hard enough he could read her mind. They were still sharp with intelligence in his mutilated face but Meaghan could see that he was once as good looking as his son. He had a thick head of white hair cut short to frame his head.

"Dad, this is Meaghan...my girlfriend," Dean said. There was an ever so slight tremor to his voice that Meaghan only noticed because she knew him well. She glanced at him briefly and then back at his father.

"It's nice to meet you Mr. Wesson. Dean talks about you all the time," she said.

"Not all the time," Dean said in protest looking at her.

"Yeah okay not all the time. Sometimes he talks about himself too," Meaghan teased grinning back at Dean – for a moment forgetting where she was. She started briefly when she remembered and looked back at Dean's father to see him smiling slightly. She was grateful for that but didn't take it for granted.

She cleared her throat and stepped forward. "Mr. Wesson, Dean might have told you that I'm a doctor?" she waited to see if there would be any response. Mr. Wesson inclined his head briefly in acknowledgment and she continued.

"Well I was telling him about this technology that might improve your quality of life and he suggested that I run it by you. So here goes," Meaghan said taking a deep breath and explaining about the robotics and how it worked. Dean's father watched her lips as she spoke and he seemed to understand what she was saying but she didn't know if it was possible for him to respond.

She told him that she'd spoken to the relevant people, at Dean's request and they'd indicated a willingness to work with the Wessons on this. Normally at this stage she would ask if the patient had any questions but in this case she didn't know if there was any way for him to ask. So she turned to look at Dean for guidance. Just then Poppy blew into the room like a hurricane.

"What are you doing in here?" she demanded of Meaghan as if she'd sneaked into the house uninvited.

"Mother. You remember my *girlfriend* Meaghan don't you?" Dean said moving between his mother and Meaghan.

"No, I can't say that I do," Poppy said still glaring at Meaghan. "As far as I know your girlfriend's name is Samantha."

Dean rolled his eyes, "Mother, Meaghan has a proposal that might help dad. Would you like to stow your crap and listen?" he asked making Meaghan hide a smile. Poppy looked totally shocked and Jeffrey looked amused.

"Well, I see she's dragging you down into the gutter with her. You never used to speak to me like that."

"You used have more respect for my friends," Dean countered.

They glared at each other as if they were in a Mexican stand off and Meaghan knew she had to do something.

"Er so what should I tell the Brain Lab people? Would you like to see if this initiative would work for you?" she asked Jeffrey. She could see his eyes lighten in amusement as if he knew exactly what she was doing. He nodded his head slightly, more of a lowering and raising of his lashes actually.

Dean turned to smile at his father. "I have a good feeling about this dad, pretty soon you'll be riding around saying 'Come with me if you want to live'," Dean had Arnold's accent down and Meaghan had to stop herself from giggling. Jeffrey smiled his amusement and Poppy looked like she wanted to protest but didn't know about what.

"Well we should leave you to rest. I'm sure Dean will keep you updated," Meaghan said shifting her legs in a way that said she wanted to get moving. Dean took the hint and took her hand, nodding at his father and ignoring his mother, he led her out.

"Well that was only about half as bad as I thought it would be," Meaghan said when they'd exited the building.

Dean shrugged, "I don't know. I think you were brilliant."

"You're biased," Meaghan protested.

Dean stopped and took her lips with his, kissing her thoroughly.

"Yes. I am," he said.

Chapter 8

Poppy walked into the offices of Drs. Dreyfuss and Dreyfuss, bypassing the receptionist who made only a token attempt to stop her – she was well known in that office – and proceeded to barge into Dr. Dreyfuss senior's office like a whirlwind of temper. Luckily the doctor was between patients so no-one other than himself was there to witness the dressing down he was getting by one of his more influential clients. It was only because she *was* influential that Dr. Dreyfuss did not have her thrown out of his office forthwith.

"How incompetent are you people here? Why did you not inform my husband that it was possible to improve his quality of life through robotics? Why did we have to hear it from some upstart gold digger trying to worm her way into my family?" she demanded. Dr. Dreyfuss had sat up at the word 'upstart', his eyes widening as he tried to make sense of Poppy's words.

"Mrs. Wesson, kindly have a seat; will you drink some water?" he tried to stall only to be bulldozed out of the way like a piece of flax weed.

"If I wanted water Dr. Dreyfuss I would have asked for it. And I will thank you not to patronize me with your smarmy tone. I have a good mind to take my business elsewhere. How could you be so remiss?" she hissed.

"Mrs. Wesson, the treatment you speak of is at an experimental stage as we speak. I cannot believe you let some charlatan turn your head like this Poppy. You know that your family's welfare is foremost in our minds at all times," Dr. Dreyfuss soothed.

Poppy allowed herself to be led to the chair and deposited in it as a glass of water was placed in her hands. Dr. Dreyfuss retreated back to his chair and sat forward, hands steepled on the table and face leaning into his hands.

"Now," he said. "Tell me all about this woman and the treatment she suggested."

*****

Said woman was ensconced in her office trying to catch up on her medical reports when a soft knock on her door distracted her. She glanced up at it, giving vague permission for whomever it was to come in and then went back to her work. Dean stuck his head in the door grinning at her.

"Hey beautiful," he said making her smile in spite of herself.

"Hey yourself. I'm working, what're you doin' here?" she said pretending to be intensely interested in the papers on her desk.

"I brought you a sandwich," he said extracting one of his hands from behind his back to present her with a brown paper bag with the name of one of her favorite deli's emblazoned on it. Her eyes brightened and she grinned happily at him.

"Oohhh! Come in, come in," she said standing up and ushering him enthusiastically into the room. He laughed at her but came in and carefully closed the door behind him; going so far as to turn the lock.

"Hmm," Meaghan said watching him.

"Yeah...so," Dean said coming forward to place the brown paper bag on the crowded table before looking up at her. "I've missed you."

"Really? From like...this morning?" Meaghan asked trying and failing to disguise her smug undertone.

Dean shrugged, unapologetic, "I'm needy like that."

"You're telling me," Meaghan said pushing her chair back so she could walk around the desk to him. She placed her hand gently on his ass and squeezed, face impassive. "How is work?" she asked kneading his ass cheek as she did so.

"Umm," Dean managed to get out, his reddening face turned slightly away from her; the better to bite his lip and grimace in helpless arousal.

"Good?" she inquired transferring her hand to his other cheek.

"Uh," Dean replied bending slightly forward so his ass was more firmly ensconced in her hand. She obliged by increasing the pressure in her kneading, and changing tactics slightly by running her hand up and down his crack.

"I'll take that as a yes," she said, her voice still cool and impassive as if she did nothing more than hold a casual conversation with a co-worker. Then her kneading began to get more intense, a little bit desperate, harder...and Dean's moaning got loud, mouth open, head thrown back. "Wow. You are enjoying this aren't you?" Meaghan whispered throatily in his ear. Dean could do nothing but groan some more and lean back into her hand. Her other hand ghosted up his back, prying his shirt loose from his pants and then burrowing inside to caress his naked back. Dean was making some sounds that would indicate his extreme pleasure in what she was doing, although really, she wasn't doing much except touching him a little; maybe running her nails against the sensitive skin below his shoulder and tracing the width of those shoulders in reverent wonder.

"Meaghan," he whispered and everything that he wanted was in her name. she reached her hands forward beneath his shirt to cradle his chest and play with his nipples. He groaned as his hand reached up to snag one of hers and urge it lower to the tent in his pants.

"Ohh," she murmured sounding pleased. "I love it when you want me in the most inappropriate places," she whispered in his ear making him laugh breathlessly.

"I want you everywhere," he breathed back at her and thrust forward into the circle her hands made around him. Meaghan's other hand crept behind to grasp his ass again and she kneaded him as he thrust forward into her other hand. She was content to get him off like that but as fast as a whirlwind, before she even had the wherewithal to understand what he was doing, he had turned the tables. She was bent over her own desk with her little red skirt riding above her tush which was thrust out, exposed to the elements since she wasn't wearing any panties. She did that sometimes, just to air things out but Dean gave a pleased laugh as if she'd done it strictly for his benefit. She felt him seeking, penis poking against her ass and her thigh before finding its way between her legs and pressing slowly into her. She closed her eyes, the better to enjoy the sensation of being widened and filled; possessed by Dean in a way that was all encompassing and yet empowering. He made that tiny sound of surrender he always made when he was wedged deep inside her and she couldn't help but feel a small thrill of triumph...every single time. She was dripping wet and ready, her body swollen with need and she needed him to fuck her hard. He seemed to realize this because he withdrew fully from her and then thrust deep into her again, not sparing her at all. He did it again...and again and she could feel that core of heat inside her spreading and swelling, ready to swallow her up, she could hardly wait. But suddenly, inexplicably, he slowed down. Talking was out of the question but she uttered an incoherent sound of protest.

"I...give me a minute or I'll come right this minute. Just keep perfectly still," he said holding her hips tight so she couldn't wriggle under him, much as she wanted to. She gave him the time he asked for but the curious core of heat continued to grow, filling her mind with urgency and desperation, wanting to be released so it could run rampant all over her body and leave her weak and shaking. Her lips let out a small sound of need and suddenly Dean was shuddering behind her, his seed filling her up as he let out pained groans and shook to completion. His body flopped forward onto her back and she shook her head in negation.

"No," she protested.

"I told you not to move," he chided. Then he withdrew from her and flipped her over depositing her legs on his shoulders and burying his face between her legs.

She gasped. "What are you doing?"

"Whaoifhooi?" was the mumbling she heard as his tongue touched parts of her she never expected to be in *anyone's* mouth? A white hot bolt of pleasure streaked across her body as his tongue landed on the delicate flesh inside her most secrets parts. His magical tongue circled that piece of flesh, making Meaghan leak everywhere and then he *sucked* and Meaghan couldn't hold the sound in anymore. She screamed out loud and then promptly held her hand to her mouth in mortification. Dean remained undaunted, though she could feel him smile against her sensitive skin. She could feel the ball of heat spreading, permeating every cell in her body, eliminating all other stimuli – then her vision went white and she felt herself float away into the ceiling, her body light as a feather....

She came to, hearing pounding on her door and Dean straightening her clothing.

"Dr. Leonard?" a deep voice asked urgently from the other side of the door. "Is everything alright?"

Meaghan absolutely froze for a moment before opening her mouth and attempting to get something out. "Uh, er...yes everything is fine. I'm sorry, I thought I saw a rat," she gasped breathlessly, hoping whomever it was would go away and leave her to her mortification in peace.

"You sure?" the voice asked not sounding convinced.

"I'm sure. Thank you for your concern," she said. Dean had put her clothes back in respectable order but the room *reeked* of sex and she wasn't ready to face a disciplinary committee or even just the damage to her reputation if whoever was behind that door found out what was going on here. She glanced at Dean, expecting him to be looking as embarrassed as she felt but his face was impassive, though there seemed to be a bit of a smug smile playing on his face. She punched him in the arm just on general principles but all it did was widen his smile.

"Okay then, I'll go now," the voice said seemingly waiting for her relieved acquiescence before walking away. She tried to glare at Dean though her body was feeling a bit too languid to completely pull it off.

"What'd you do that for?" she asked as if she really minded.

Dean quirked his brow at her. "Are you trying to claim you didn't enjoy it?" he challenged.

"Of course I enjoyed it," Meaghan said like it was the most obvious thing in the world, "that is so not the point."

"What's the point?" Dean asked running his hands up and down Meaghan's sides. She sighed shaking her head at his obtuseness.

"Nothing," she said moving away from him. "Did you bring your own sandwich cause you're not sharing mine," she declared picking up the paper bag.

Dean smiled, "Actually I was just dropping that off, I have a lunch meeting with a new investor – he wants to woo me into a partnership I think."

"Really? As in he wants to buy into Wesson Diamonds?" Meaghan asked exactly as if she actually cared.

"I'm not sure. I think he has mines in South Africa and wants to speak to us about distribution," he said as he tucked in his shirt.

"Okay well," Meaghan said coming to straighten his collar and check that he had no untoward stains. "I think you're ready for your close up now," she said.

Dean smiled, leaned forward and kissed her. "I'll see you later."

"Yes dear," Meaghan smiled back at him. He turned around and walked out with a small wave as she dug into her sandwich. It was her favorite kind, chicken, cheese and onions.

"I have the best boyfriend in the world," she said to no-one and then froze; hoping frantically that whoever had heard her scream was not still loitering in the corridor. Seeing Dean walk out of her office would just put a different (more accurate) slant on her screaming and lord knew she did not need that shit. Especially not at work when she was in the midst of her residency and trying her best to impress her supervisor, Dr. Conrad Shelley who also happened to be the director at her locum job where she fulfilled her lifelong dream to do community outreach. She stood up again and opened her door tentatively, peeking out to see who was in the corridor. A solitary cleaner was moving a mop from side to side at the other end of the corridor and two patients were sitting on a bench outside a closed door that she *thought* led to phlebotomy

but that was it. She studied the patients, wondering if they'd heard

anything but they seemed too absorbed in their own pain to notice

much else.

Meaghan pulled her head back into the room and shut the door,

flopping onto the couch to eat her sandwich and hope for the best.

*****

Dean was slightly late for lunch but he just could not give less of a

fuck right now. The person he was meeting wanted something from

him not the other way around. He was fine with making them work

for it. His team of private investigators had already looked into the

firm behind this meeting known as De Beers. They'd uncovered a

few questionable practices in the past but the company was

currently under new management. Dean licked his lips tasting

Meaghan on his tongue – interspersed with the salty bitter taste of

his own come that he'd licked out of her center. He could feel himself getting hard again just thinking about it and adjusted his pants to accommodate his swelling member. Just then he spotted his hosts standing up at their table waiting for him; looked like they'd spotted him too. Hopefully his arousal was not immediately apparent...

To his surprise the contact who had called him, Mr. Van der Roodt was not alone; he was with a tall attractive woman who was giving him the eye...and the smile. Dean smirked internally wondering what kind of con these people were trying to run. Did they think they could seduce him into falling in line with their wishes? Had they not heard of the latest scandal making the rounds among the country club set, about him and the *totally unsuitable female* he'd taken up with? Dean smiled to himself and walked toward them, mentally daring them to do their worst.

"Mr. Wesson, a pleasure to finally meet you," the white guy he assumed was Van der Roodt said. Dean nodded his acknowledgment and then turned to the female whose ethnicity was less certain. She was tall, almost his height, with auburn hair that was possibly not natural. Her dusky complexion was perfectly clear of blemish and her honey brown eyes stared at him with interest.

"May I present my companion...Ms. Adriana Stuijt? She's our head of A&R," guy said.

"Interesting name," Dean murmured.

Adriana smiled at him and then sat down so they could sit as well. A waiter appeared as if by magic placing a bread basket on the table and distributing menus. Dean glanced at it, trying to find something he was interested in eating. Nothing jumped out at him; in fact if he was being honest he would rather be in Meaghan's hospital office sharing her deli sandwich than here at this fancy restaurant trying to choose between foie gras, or duck confit. He was inclined to go with the latter since he was pretty sure this restaurant didn't do sandwiches. Maybe he could take a doggy bag back to Meaghan; food was just that much more fun to eat with her in the room.

Once orders had been taken and the waiter had brought their food along with an appropriately expensive bottle of white wine, Van der Roodt fired his opening salvo.

"First of all, allow me to invite you to call me Jan. Mr Van der Roodt is quite a mouthful and I'd like us to be on friendlier terms than that," he said smiling.

Dean made a non-committal sound. He wasn't that easily won over.

Jan continued to speak as if Dean had acquiesced. "As I'm sure you know, we're one of the biggest suppliers of rough diamonds and we're looking for a new partner in the distribution process here in America who undertakes the process of cutting and polishing, basically turning our rough diamonds into jewels. Your company has shown great resilience in the wake of the financial crisis and with the peaceful handover of power from your father to you without any major fluctuations. We would like to congratulate you on your stability and offer you the opportunity to work with one of the best in class in the business. We can all profit insanely from this partnership," he finished.

Dean just looked at him, nodding his head to indicate understanding but otherwise not indicating in any way whether he was in favor or not of this idea. Adriana leaned forward so her cleavage was peeking out of the v-neck of her red business suit.

"Mr. Wesson, may I call you Dean?" she asked in a soft sultry tone and continued speaking before he had a chance to refuse. "We would like to invite you to a benefit that De Beers is holding at the Museum of Modern Art. Proceeds will go to casualties of the Blood Diamond trade. I'm sure that is a cause you could get behind. And it would give you a chance to really get to know who we are," she said.

Dean perked up for the first time in the conversation. "I see. And when is this event?"

Jan and Adrianna exchanged muted triumphant glances and Dean pretended not to notice.

"It's on the tenth of next month," Adriana said putting her hand strategically on the table, near to his. "I'd be honored to escort you to the event," she added searching his face hopefully. Dean mouth twisted in a wry smile.

"I think I can find my own plus one. Thank you for asking though," he said.

Adriana sat back, visibly disappointed. "Well...anyway. We look forward to seeing you there." Her accent had thickened, with more emphasis on the consonants and a slightly sing song cadence to her speech. Dean still couldn't place her origins but he guessed that it was also at least partly from southern Africa. He considered asking her straight out but didn't want to seem prejudiced. His glance flipped to her hair, assessing it for natural curliness but it was straightened either artificially or naturally; Dean couldn't really tell. He jerked back suddenly, wondering why he was so interested in Adriana's hair anyway, or her ethnicity...it was none of his business. He stood up, preparing to leave and they stood up with him.

"Well this has been interesting. Have your people call my people to set up a more formal presentation."

Jan inclined his head. "Will do. And we'll send you that official invite for the benefit," he hesitated slightly. "Will there be a plus one?" he asked diffidently.

Dean quirked his eyebrow. "Why of course," he said with a smirk. Jan inclined his head again in acknowledgment and then Dean turned around and left. He felt the need to get away from these people for some reason.

*****

"Hey Meaghan, what was going on in your office earlier?" Nurse Rachette asked her as she came to drop off the reports at reception.

"What do you mean?" she asked her, feeling her face warm.

"I mean...there's a rumor that a little raunchiness took place there this afternoon. True or false and is it that white guy who keeps coming to see you?" the nurse asked leaning forward confidentially. Her and Meaghan were not really friends; more like familiar acquaintances. Meaghan had cultivated her because it was necessary to have a nurse on your side if one was to survive the grueling schedule they were under. She wasn't sure though, if spilling about her personal life was really merited to keep nurse Rachette's goodwill. After all it was exactly none of her business what Meaghan got up to behind closed doors. Granted these closed doors were at work but still...the theory applied.

"I don't know what you're talking about," she said, signing her reports in with a glance at the nurse and then walking off. She'd let her make of that what she would.

"Hi Megs," Mr. Henley waved to her as she walked past the waiting room. He'd taken to coming for his diabetes medication at this clinic ever since she started working here.

"Hey Mr. Henley, alright?" she asked stopping to exchange a word.

"Great," he replied grinning, preening a bit that the big shot doctor had stopped to speak to him. "How is that boyfriend of yours?" he asked.

It was Meaghan's turn to grin. "Great," she said.

Mr. Henley gave her two thumbs up and she went on, continuing with her day with as minimum of fuss as she could manage in the circumstances.

Chapter 9

"We have an invitation to attend a benefit next month," Dean told her over dinner much to her intense surprise.

"What?" she asked. "Since when do 'we' go to benefits? Isn't that more something you'd do with your mom?"

"Yeah before when you were my dirty little secret," Dean said with a sly grin. "But now that we're 'out' I don't see any reason why we can't go together."

Meaghan swallowed, forking some spaghetti into her mouth and chewing and swallowing thoughtfully before she answered. "I suppose technically you're correct."

"There's no technically about it," he said a bit curtly.

"Okay so is it now mandatory that I attend these events?" she asked not really wanting to mix with his snobbish friends and endure their judgment. It would be easier if Bain attended such events but he was also eager to avoid his set's arbitrary judgments so he tended to ignore these society events too.

"Not mandatory no. But I thought it way past time you were seen on my arm. Don't you *want* people to know we're together?" Dean was frowning at her.

Meaghan took a deep breath; she didn't know how to tell Dean about her reservations without making him feel like she was rejecting or denigrating his lifestyle. Which was pretty ironic because these things usually ran the other way around. *She* was the one who grew up in a trailer park; she had no right not to want to rub shoulders with the rich and famous of New York City now that her handsome billionaire boyfriend wanted to parade her on his arm...it was decidedly awkward not to be enthusiastic about this invitation. So Meaghan tried to dredge up some eagerness from the depths of her being.

"Of course I want people to know," she said concentrating on wrapping spaghetti around her fork. Dean was staring at her and then shook his head.

"It doesn't seem like it," he said.

Meaghan stopped playing with her fork. "Well I'm sorry you feel that-" she began to say staring at him.

"Don't play with me Meaghan," Dean cut in rather curtly, badly startling Meaghan. She dropped her fork onto her plate, mouth slightly open as she stared at him speechlessly. She picked up her fork again and forked some spaghetti into her mouth, waiting impassively for him to continue. The silence stretched uncomfortably and Meaghan felt compelled to fill it.

"You'd do very well working with ISIS. Interrogation technique is on fleek," she murmured with a small smile. Dean smiled reluctantly back but didn't let her attempt to lighten the mood distract him. He continued to stare at her with narrowed eyes until she put her fork down again and stared back at him with a sigh.

"Okay fine, I am a little nervous about...all this. I'm not sure how wise it would be to rock the boat now. I mean we've done the essential bit; your dad and mom know who I am to you. That's the important thing right?" she said.

"So you *are* ashamed," Dean pressed.

"I'm not. *Really,*" she insisted as she saw his hurt disbelief. "I just... it's hard. People have expectations of me that I either don't meet or surpass depending on what they were anticipating. I feel like there's a spotlight on me every time I'm around your friends – and most of them knew me from high school. I imagine it'll be ten thousand times worse when it's mostly a bunch of rich snobby strangers I've never met."

Dean continued to stare at her in disbelief for a moment and then he barked a laugh, "That's funny."

"Why is that funny?" Meaghan asked preparing to be indifferent.

"It's funny because after everything you've been through in your life, you're intimidated by a bunch of tame blue bloods?" he asked with a smirk.

"Tame my ass," Meaghan murmured in an aggrieved undertone. "Y'all are a bunch of sharks."

"Ooooh, poor Meaghan scared of the scary blue blood sharks with the long teeth," Dean sing songed, making fun of her.

"Well I am," Meaghan said firmly chin in the air, "and I am not ashamed."

"Well you should be; that is totally pathetic. You should know that the head of A&R, this new firm, already tried to hit on me. So if you want me to go all alone and *expose* us to the danger of having my head turned…" he threatened.

"Please. If I have to watch you like a Doberman this relationship ain't worth it," Meaghan countered.

"Well too bad. You're going, whether you like it or not. It's part of your girlfriend duties." Dean declared.

"Great," Meaghan replied but not like she meant it.

*****

"Bain, you have to come for this benefit," Meaghan said desperately.

"I do?" Bain asked watching the lady doing his nails closely because sometimes they removed too much cuticle for his taste.

"Yes!" Meaghan said almost pulling her own fingers out of her manicurist's hands causing her to utter a weak protest. Meaghan turned to her. "Sorry Mei," she said before returning her attention to Bain.

"Why?" Bain asked as he had another beautician place cucumbers on his eyes. He was forced to lie back and close them much to his chagrin because he could *feel* his manicurist taking too much off his nails. "Not too much okay?" he said warningly.

"Yes sah Mr. Bain," the manicurist said. Meaghan smiled at the fake Asian accent. Just last week she'd ran across Mei at the train station talking in fast and furious Brooklynese to this other beautician. She'd ducked away so they didn't see her; no need to embarrass anyone needlessly after all; and she guessed she could understand pandering to stereotypes if it helped one to make their daily bread. She turned back to Bain.

"Look, you know everyone's going to be looking at me, judging me, talking about me behind my back...I need an ally I can count on. Please Bain," she wheedled.

"I thought Dean had your back...or don't you trust him?" Bain needled in return.

Meaghan just gave him a long sidelong glance to let him know what she thought of his jabs. Bain and Dean barely got along.

"Please. Don't make me invoke the best friend contract article nine, line eight," she pleaded.

"Oh fine, if you're going to bring the friend contract into it," Bain said sounding aggrieved. "But I'm bringing Daniel," he warned.

"You do that," Meaghan said. Daniel was Bain's stripper boyfriend and even though he was perfectly house trained and knew how to behave in public, he was still a very flamboyant gay man who knew exactly how attractive he was. It didn't exactly make for shrinking violet type behavior. Meaghan was happy to hear that Daniel would be coming. Not only did they have excellent rapport, but he would be even more of a misfit than she would be. They could watch each other's backs.

Beauty regime completed, it was time for their weekly dinner. Bain had turned it into an elaborate production in the last year, mostly to discourage any gate crashing from their respective love interests. Neither Daniel nor Dean was interested in hanging out at an Asian nail salon during rush hour or dressing up in elaborate costume to go have dinner at *La Trattoria* where they were likely not to be joined by the proprietor, Luigi, who may or may not be half in love with Bain. Meaghan and Bain enjoyed it though; it was an escape from 'real' life and a chance to catch up that they wouldn't otherwise have what with their busy professional and personal lives. Meaghan was busy juggling the attempt to become a surgeon with walking the fine line between being Dean's girlfriend and not setting off an international incident by saying the wrong thing at the wrong place at the exact right time. Bain was busy building his architectural business by altering the skyline of New York while artfully dodging Daniel's attempts to get him to the proverbial altar. He greeted the announcement that yet another state had legalized gay marriage with trepidation.

Being together was like sanctuary from a world that expected so much more of them than they were ready to give.

"What's the big deal with this benefit anyway? Is it your first?" Bain asked over a dinner of delicious lasagna and Luigi's own vintage of wine.

"Well yeah, of course it's my first," Meaghan began before Bain stopped her by imitating a buzzer sound.

"Nope you remember when we were seventeen I took you as my date to that stray dogs benefit?" Bain said.

"It wasn't a stray dog benefit," Meaghan said laughing, "it was a rescue dog one."

"Po-ta-to, Po-tah-to," Bain replied dismissively. "The point is this isn't your first time hobnobbing with the gentry."

"Yeah but it *is* my first time as Dean's girlfriend," Meaghan qualified.

"And that makes it different why? He's not exactly Pygmalion," Bain said contemptuously.

"And Galatea I am not. Still...he already has all this anxiety about his dad and his company stocks; his mother already hates me. I guess we're more Romeo and Juliet without the teenage angst and suicide," Meaghan said speculatively.

Bain laughed. "Please, you guys are straight out Acontius and Cydippe," he said. Meaghan inclined her head to the side.

"I'm not sure I know that one," she said.

Bain sighed and rolled his eyes. "That's what you get for sleeping through literature classes...So the highlights; Acontius was a young man from Chios who, at a festival at Delos, fell in love with the Athenian Cydippe. He threw a coin at her, and she picked it up and read, 'I swear by the temple of Artemis that I shall marry Acontius...' By saying it aloud, she was obligated to marry him. This myth reiterates how tradition—and male aspirations—took precedence over female wishes, whatever they may or may not be."

"So you're saying Dean's wishes take precedence over mine?" Meaghan asked in disbelief.

"I'm saying you're giving yourself anxiety attacks over a goddamned party Megs. A party." Bain emphasized looking Meaghan in the eye. "Since when do you give a fuck about these things?"

Meaghan opened her mouth and then closed it again. She was saved from having to make an immediate response by Luigi who brought the dessert himself. It was tiramisu with gelato and it made Meaghan's mouth water even though she'd been sure not two seconds ago that she couldn't eat anymore.

Bain didn't say a word; just let her tuck in to her sweets until she couldn't pretend to be absorbed anymore.

"I don't know what's happening to me. I know this isn't me," she said quietly.

"It's easy to lose yourself when you think you're in love," Bain conceded.

"I don't *think* Bain. I know."

"No, I know you know...I just...I'm saying he's your first love and it's easy to get lost in that."

"I don't want to get lost," Meaghan said putting down her spoon and wiping sauce off the side of her mouth.

"I know you don't. That's what I'm here for," Bain reassured her, hand covering hers comfortingly.

"I still need you to come to the benefit," Meaghan said smiling.

"You know I'm there for you honey," Bain said spooning more chocolate gelato into his mouth.

*****

Dean walked into his parent's mansion nodding in passing at the butler. He'd called as soon as Poppy had left the house because

Dean wanted to see his father but he needed to avoid his mother. She was beyond tiresome with her tirades about Meaghan and he just didn't want to hear it anymore. The butler, Reeves, had informed him that Poppy was out for lunch followed by a Daughters of the American Revolution meeting. That meant Dean had at least four hours before Poppy would be expected back.

"Hallo father," he breezed as he stepped into his father's room.

Jeffrey Wesson smiled delightedly at his son, he was hooked up to a machine that helped him articulate what he wanted to say but he was still learning to control it, so it was exhausting. He tried to limit its usage to very necessary communications and just continued with facial gestures otherwise.

"How are you feeling?" Dean asked as he came to sit by his father's bed and take his hand. Jeffrey shrugged as if to say 'so-so' and Dean squeezed his hand.

"It'll get better," he said reassuringly. Jeffrey's eyes drifted past Dean to the door and then back to Dean again. He lifted his brow.

"Who? Mom? Gone," Dean said with a small side smile. Jeffrey's brow cleared and then he beetled his brows as if censuring Dean.

"Yeah I know. I need to do something about that situation but I don't see what I can do right now short of doing what she wants me to do," Dean protested the unspoken plea to get along with his mother. Jeffrey unbeetled his brow as if to ask why he couldn't do *that.*

"I love her dad, this isn't just some teenage rebellion thing or whatever mother thinks is going on. I can't go back to Samantha. Can you imagine meeting mother and then going back to whomever you used to flirt with before you met her?" Dean asked with a bit of a smirk.

Jeffrey's eyes grew wry with agreement.

"Anyway dad, I wanted to tell you about the meeting I had with the De Beers people. I know their reputation is solid but their methods were just the tiniest bit shady and I wanted to run the whole thing by you to see if you agree with me or if I am over-reacting," Dean said.

Jeffrey nodded as if urging him to continue so that is what Dean did. He explained about the meeting and what his private investigator had found out about the company and its directors.

"It seems a pretty solid deal although I have scheduled a meeting with several of their collaborators just to see if they live up to the reputation," Dean said.

"Board of directors?" the computer microphone intoned.

"Yeah, the board of directors is on board with us partnering up with them, subject to several quid pro quos as laid out by the legal and finance departments. We're scheduled for that meet after the benefit," Dean said.

Jeffrey raised his brows in inquiry.

"Oh yeah, I forgot to tell you about that. De Beers invited us to a benefit they're holding at the Museum of Modern Art. Something to do with helping the victims of Blood Diamonds. It's good PR as well as a worthy cause."

Jeffrey nodded his approval and then computer intoned, "Keep me posted."

Dean checked his watch. "Dad, I'd love to stay longer but I really don't want to run into Poppy so I'm out of here. I'll see you soon."

Jeffrey frowned again as Dean looked up at him.

"I'm really sorry dad. I wish things could be better but for now…this is how things have gotta be," he said. The frown didn't leave Jeffrey's face and Dean tried to figure out why.

"Language" the computer voice intoned.

Jeffrey stared uncomprehendingly at his father, wondering what the hell he was talking about. He ran over what he'd just said, looking for swear words or whatever it was that caused his father to disapprove. The frown on his face slowly cleared as he realized that he was talking like Meaghan, his words full of the cadences of Queens. He'd been spending so much time with her, and with her mother, and her family friend Mr. Henley that he was starting to talk like them.

"I'm sorry," he murmured to his father and then walked out quietly. As he tripped down the stairs to his car he laughed softly to himself. He needed to watch himself in the future around both his parents. He didn't need to alienate his father as well.

*****

Hey Dean darling, would you mind if we took a rain check on the whole Friday night date night thing? I gotta go home.

www.SaucyRomanceBooks.com/RomanceBooks

Meaghan texted Dean as she got into work so she would have time to deal with all his sulky refusals before the work day was at an end. She did not want him coming down to the hospital to get her after work; she had a solid plan that involved taking the train home and spending the evening with Mr. Henley at his auto shop. She figured if she was going to 'find herself' it was a great place to start. She'd spent a good portion of her childhood studying in his office while classic rock blasted from the speakers. He'd shaped her taste in music and was responsible for at least a quarter of her values. Her mother was at work; she had the night shift at the hospital so the house was empty but Mr. Henley stayed at his shop sometimes until one in the morning. They could catch up; maybe she could read as he worked on the cars. Do his books for old times' sake... Maybe she would even meet some other interesting customer looking for a quick fix for their ride that they didn't want their rich friends to know about. Meaghan smiled remembering in vivid detail the day that she'd met Dean for the first time. He'd driven in with his damaged Lamborghini and a wad of cash. Mr. Henley had been busy so it was left to Meaghan to greet him. She hadn't known who he was but he remembered *her*. She could still recall their conversation quite clearly.

She had been working late one night - or rather she'd gotten caught up reading the Iliad while Bon Jovi blasted from the speakers and she didn't want to move - when a new customer drove into the garage. She had looked down from the window in the office that was at the top of a flight of stairs and saw that the garage below her was deserted. Mr. Henley had said something about going out for a smoke; no smoking was allowed in the garage because it was a fire hazard and it was late so no-one else seemed to be around. She had wondered what she should do; it wasn't like she could help the customer with his car...

He had alighted from the vehicle and Meaghan had got a load of his full head of hair as he looked around for someone to help him. He looked lost. The car was too expensive for this neighborhood and the guy was too well dressed. Meaghan stood and left the office, descending the stairs self-consciously as the guy watched her come to him. She guessed there was nothing else to look at really, but still she wished he would look away.

"Hi. Can I help you?" she'd asked him. Being up close and personal with him, and standing on the same level had brought home to her how tall he was; and well built. But not as old as she'd first thought when she saw his clothes. No, he was closer to her age than the mid twenties she'd assumed at his outfit. Fitted khaki slacks and blue fitted shirt that looked tailor made for him. His dark hair was windswept and untidy but that could have been because he'd just alighted from a convertible...Lamborghini Aventador if she wasn't mistaken. His green eyes were so intent on her that she felt like squirming but drew herself up instead and looked back at him.

"Where do I know you from?" he'd asked ignoring her question.

"What? I'm pretty sure I don't know you," she had replied and then wondered if that was rude and if Mr. Henley would be mad at her for being brusque with his customers.

"Yes. I've seen you somewhere," he said looking her up and down. And then his eyes fell on the book in her hand. It was emblazoned with 'The Dalton School' along its sleeve which was facing him. The frown cleared from his face.

"Oh you're the scholarship chick in my biological sciences class aren't you?" he had said. "You look different without the mountain of books you're usually carrying."

Meaghan had been so bemused with him; it had been a surreal night and she smiled to think of it. That sixteen year old that she was had been a lot more self-possessed than Meaghan felt these days; granted her life was also much less complicated so she probably didn't have much to stress about except getting good grades. Outsiders might imagine that living in a trailer park gave her lots of materiel for angst and depression but she got on with her

mother, they had food to eat and beds to sleep in. She took care of

her own schooling by getting a scholarship. Life had been pretty

good.

Chapter 10

"We have to go shopping," Bain said.

"Time to break out the emergency black card?" Meaghan asked.

"Nope. Because I have a perfectly good non-emergency black card

we can use," Bain said.

"Fuck that. If anyone is buying Meaghan clothes for the benefit it's

going to be me," Dean cut in, startling Meaghan quite badly

because she hadn't been aware that he was listening. Last she

looked he was across the room with Smith, his best friend and Bella,

Smith's sister. Bella and her husband-to-be had decided on a joint

bachelor/bachelorette party so as to eliminate the potential for

jealous fits and/or misunderstandings. It was a small party with

Bella and Corbett's close friends in attendance at a private room at

the Midtown Hilton. A few faces were familiar to Meaghan from

school and some were well known celebrity faces she'd seen in

magazines; Bain and Daniel as well as Dean and Smith were the only ones she knew personally. Thankfully Samantha was at a shoot on the Cayman Islands so there was no need to worry about her showing up. Meaghan had *almost* forgotten Samantha's existence in the last few months in the wake of everything else going on in her life; but being in a room with a bevy of Samantha's friends was forcefully reminding her that the feud with Dean's ex-girlfriend was *not* over.

She'd retired to a corner with Bain who was sulking a little bit because the same bevy of women were taking *a lot* of interest in Daniel who had come to the party from work and therefore was wearing a tight black t-shirt and black jeans that held on to everything. With his long blonde hair and gray eyes he looked like a demi-god come to earth to fornicate with virgins. No-one was claiming to be a virgin in that group but they were down for the fornicating anyway. Daniel had eyes only for Bain anyway, but his mother had raised him to be polite so he was patiently smiling and flirting with the group because they were Bain's friends. Bain left him to it and he knew what Daniel was doing; nevertheless it brought back echoes of Luigi leaving him for a woman and that made him itchy. Hence his hunching in the corner with arms and legs crossed. When Meaghan saw how he was sitting, she came across to him immediately to distract him with prospects of shopping and new outfits. It was a relief to get away from the cattiness of the women and the slightly sleazy sidelong glances she was getting from the males. She felt like fresh meat on her first day in jail. It was nerve wracking.

Dean and Bain were still bickering over who was going to pay for her clothes for the benefit and she was inclined to let them battle it out but if her relationship with the former was going to go anywhere, he really was going to have to learn to play nice with the latter. With that in mind, encouraging bickering was probably not wise. So Meaghan stepped in to inform them both that she would be buying her own dress.

"What?" they said in unison.

"I will be buying my own dress," she intoned solemnly as she stared at them both.

"Meaghan," Dean began to protest.

"My mother is already on it okay? She has something great lined up for me already," Meaghan lied.

Dean opened his mouth, thought about what he was about to say and then closed it again. Bain just glared at her.

"Girl, we're going shopping. I don't care if you already have the perfect dress, I need a suit and you're coming with me," Bain said.

"What about Daniel?" she asked.

"Daniel can do his own damn shopping. We ain't joined at the hip," Bain said. Meaghan turned to look at Daniel busy flirting away with girls...sometimes she felt sorry for him – other times she was resigned. After all, Daniel knew what he was getting himself into by now. Or he should. And she really did want to go shopping with Bain, he was so much fun making fun of fellow shoppers and choosing the exact right color for her and for himself. But if Dean heard that she went shopping with Bain he'd take it personally and it would just blow up into yet another thing to hold against each other.

She snaked her arm through Dean's and led him away.

"Why you always fighting with my best fwend?" she asked pouting.

"Why's he always trying to rain on my parade?" he countered.

"I promise you, he isn't," Meaghan tried to protest.

"Sure sure, he just tries to cock block me all the time out of the goodness of his heart," Dean said nastily.

"Wow, Dean Wesson using words like cock block...you been spending time with the wrong people my man," Meaghan said.

Dean laughed, "Funny you should say that."

Meaghan looked quizzically at him but he just shook his head and took her over to the drinks table to ply her with more wine. Meaghan took it gladly; she knew they were headed back into the fray from there and she needed all the Dutch courage she could get.

"Ooh, Dean and his new girlfriend," Bella smiled as Dean led her back where she and Corbett were holding court. "You guys are just...joined at the hip aren't you?"

Dean pretended to study their hips to ascertain the veracity of this statement. "Doesn't look like it," he told her at last.

Meaghan snorted with laughter and one of the other girls, a tall thin blonde that Meaghan might have seen somewhere or maybe she was just a generic looking specimen, glared at her like she'd committed a major faux pas.

"How long have you guys been together?" she asked, an edge to her voice.

Meaghan shrugged, "It seems like forever."

"Aww, you're sweet," Dean said and kissed her cheeks. He turned to Meaghan. "We should probably get home. Didn't you say you have an early shift tomorrow?"

Meaghan stared at him because she was pretty sure he knew that she was off tomorrow seeing as she'd worked a double shift for three days this week. He glared meaningfully at her so she nodded her head dumbly. "Uh huh," she said.

"Okay then, we'll go," Dean said threading his hand with hers and pulling her toward the door with a quick wave at Smith, Bella and Corbett.

"Can I tell Bain I'm leaving?" Meaghan asked.

"No," Dean said shortly.

"Okay," Meaghan said while trying to catch Bain's eye across the room. He was distracted as Daniel had managed to get away from the girls and was now straddling him, so he didn't see them leave. Meaghan decided she'd text him later and followed Dean down to the car.

"What was that?" she asked as he opened the door for her.

"What was what?" Dean asked getting into his side.

"The whole escape from the party thing by lying about me working tomorrow."

"Oh. That," Dean said driving off.

"Yes. That," Meaghan said grinning.

"I figured you wanted out, and I wanted to be alone with you so I-" Dean shrugged.

"I see…" Meaghan said. "Well, thanks."

"Don't mention it," Dean said smiling.

He drove them to his house above his bookshop; a tiny brick apartment that nevertheless managed to be quite spacious. Perhaps it had something to do with the dearth of furniture. Apart from an L-shaped beige leather sofa facing a 61 inch flat screen TV above a fireplace the living room contained only an entire wall of books artfully arranged but not decorative. The bedroom had Dean's massive black metal four poster bed and a black and white woolen rug on the floor. He had a closet built into the wall and a massive landscape painting of a hilly field depicting a distant golfer hitting a ball into the sunset. The picture actually featured Dean himself painted by an upcoming artist he'd discovered in Central Park. It was his favorite piece though he had some expensive art pieces scattered about the apartment intermingled with street art. Hell he even had a Banksy that he'd acquired through a friend. His kitchen was state of the art though, with every possible appliance installed. Dean's secret passion was cooking though he hardly had much time to indulge.

There was an entrance to the apartment from the bookshop and another through the alley at the back. Poppy kept nagging at Dean about insecurity but he mostly ignored her. He had a state of the art security system installed and his front door was bio-metrically controlled. No-one could get in or out without his assistance; not even his housekeeper, Carmen. He was considering inputting Meaghan's details into the system so she could have a metaphorical key to his place but he wasn't sure if it was time yet. Maybe they should talk about her having a drawer first.

"Would you like a drawer in my apartment?" he asked as they climbed the stairs.

"What? Like...for my spare underwear and stuff?" she asked.

"Yeah, you know, so you can keep some clothes here. You practically live here..." he said.

"I do not. I spend maybe...three nights a week here, tops," Meaghan protested.

"It's not a competition," Dean said.

"I know it's not, I'm just sayin'…" Meaghan said, not exactly sure of exactly what she was saying. She may have had more to drink than she realized at the time.

Dean let them into the apartment and went straight to the liquor cabinet to pour them a drink.

"Er, I don't think I should drink another," Meaghan murmured.

"Okay fine, but I could use a nightcap," Dean said.

"You mind if I use your shower?" Meaghan asked.

"Mi shower e su shower," Dean replied with a smile. Meaghan smiled back reaching down to grasp the hem of her dress and pull it over her head. She dropped it on the floor like it was yesterday's news and sauntered off to the shower in just her bra and underwear, discarding the former by the door of the bedroom and entering the bathroom while taking off her panties. Dean poured out his nightcap and followed, holding the glass as if forgotten in his hand. The bathroom door was unlocked and he went in without knocking. It was a spacious room, big enough to contain a bathtub and a shower encased in a glass box. There was also a sink and a small bench on which to sit. A potted plant sat in the corner near the window so as to get enough sunlight. He could see Meaghan in the shower, the glass was slightly misted with steam but she was still visible, head thrown back, hands working up and down her body. She seemed to be enjoying the water and Dean took a seat on the bench to watch her while sipping his drink.

"Looks like fun in there," he ventured after a while.

"It is," Meaghan replied though she didn't deign to look at him.

"Want some company?" Dean asked kneading his khakis at the crotch.

Meaghan smiled. "No I'm good," she said, touching her breasts thoughtfully.

Dean unzipped his fly and dug into his boxers, breath hitching and accelerating as his hands moved.

Meaghan ran her hands down her sides, her movements obscured by the mist. Dean narrowed his eyes and stood up divesting himself of his pants and boxers and then his shirt. He walked naked toward the shower and pulled back the glass door.

"Surprise," he said as his swollen, reddened member preceded him into the shower stall.

"Oh," Meaghan said impassively. Dean pressed against her behind, rubbing gently against her.

"Ohh," he said in an entirely different tone.

"Enjoying yourself there cowboy?" Meaghan asked in amusement. She bent over slightly so she could rub her behind against his pelvis.

"Uhhhh," he groaned pushing into her even as she pressed into him. His leg came between hers and nudged her legs wider apart as his hand came down on her back to bend her lower.

"Oh I see a little doggy style in the shower huh?" she drawled.

"Got the gin and juice already," Dean replied tongue in cheek.

"Weak ass," Meaghan laughed.

Dean grabbed her ass. "Let me tell you about asses," he said reaching down to take a bite out of one of her ass cheeks. Meaghan screamed with laughter.

"Staahhp," she said but pushed her ass nearer to his face so Dean took another bite. He kneaded her ass and then widened her cheeks, running his finger up and down her crack and causing her to moan softly.

"Just do it already," she said impatiently.

"Stop, go, don't, do...you're being very confusing right now Megs my love," he said.

"A little less conversation here," Meaghan said.

Dean grasped his member, questing along her ass crack until he found the entrance he was looking for. They both groaned as he entered her; she was dripping wet inside and out so it was an easy ride. He pumped steadily into her, talking dirty the whole time.

"You like what I'm doing to you huh? I wanna fuck you all night. Wanna fuck you till you can't walk. Till you can't move. I want to do it so hard you can't walk straight for a month," he whispered into her ear as he pumped faster and faster into her as Meaghan moaned.

"Do it," she whispered spreading her legs wider to give him more access. The hot water poured on her back steadily creating a heated counter measure to the heat inside her. Dean took her entreaty as a command he needed to accomplish or die trying and her head almost smashed through the wall tiles, he was thrusting into her so hard.

"Meaghan," he whispered and her muscles wrapped tightly around him, creating a swelling, throbbing vortex which was sucking them both in.

"Do it," she said again and he surged forward, this time almost causing her a concussion for real as her head connected with the wall. His hands tightened on her hips and he pulled her to him, body stiffening as he began to shudder and release himself into her. He said her name again and that was it for her, the vortex reached out and swallowed her whole and she went willingly into it, surrendering her body and soul to the madness that was intercourse with Dean.

As they collapsed against the wall and slid down to the floor – still attached – Meaghan asked breathlessly, "Is it always like this?"

Dean didn't even pretend not to know what she meant. "You mean with other people?"

"I mean generally," Meaghan said.

Dean shrugged, "I don't know. I do know that in *my own experience* this is crazy unusual."

"In a good way or bad?" Meaghan persisted.

"Definitely good. Great in fact. I can't articulate enough how wonderful it is when you and me do it."

"Of course you could just be lying to me; there is no way for me to find out for sure."

"You know, I love that you would say that. It doesn't even occur to you to cheat does it?" Dean asked shifting slightly in a way that sent strobes of feeling along her nerve endings. She could feel him getting hard again.

"The delight in your voice is disconcerting," Meaghan observed trying to ignore the going ons within her in favor of garnering some new information.

"It's disconcerting that I'm delighted that you wouldn't cheat on me?"

"It's disconcerting that you would consider this to be a standard option and are delighted that you've come across someone who doesn't. It says something about the world you live in."

"Touché," Dean said. "You see why I'm so happy you're my girlfriend?"

"I do," Meaghan said bobbing her head. "I still feel sorry for you though."

"You do that. Just don't change," Dean said hugging her close and swirling his hips so he was even deeper inside her.

Meaghan moaned softly and straddled his thighs so she could put her hands on the floor and lift and drop herself onto his penis. He groaned leaning forward to give her more room to maneuver. She rose and fell faster onto him, making grunting sounds as she tried to satisfy the distant itch in her body that could not seem to be scratched no matter how much friction she tried to generate.

She turned around to face him, putting her hands around his neck and lifting and lowering herself on him while he held her hips lightly.

"Meaghan," he whispered but she covered his lips with hers because his voice just made the itch worse. Dean grasped her tightly around the hips, raising and lowering her onto him with increasing urgency. Their breaths were coming in hoarse, laborious and fast as their lips fused into one passionate entity.

Meaghan ground into him, gyrating her hips to get him as deep as he could go, face contorted with effort and emotion.

"Oh God, baby...save me....so good," Dean murmured incoherently spurring Meaghan on to greater effort.

"Ohh fuckkk," she whispered as she felt him inside, so deep and hungry, yet it wasn't nearly enough for her.

"It's not...it's not enough," she murmured in his ear and he surged upwards and forward, laying her down gently below him and placing her legs over his neck so he could really go to town on her on the bathroom floor. Normally Meaghan would be all sorts of disturbed by having her hair, wet, and so near the drainage system of a shower but at the moment she couldn't be bothered. She was too busy trying to get that itch scratched. She took her own legs in her hands and held them wide open so that Dean had free reign to pound her into the tiles.

"Uh uh uh," she moaned, voice getting louder with each exhalation of sound. Her muscles tightened and at last she felt the warm bubble within her burst and spread its liquid everywhere. Dean made a strained sound and then he was filling her with his seed again, jerkily pumping within her as his face twisted up in a rictus of strain and bulging veins. Meaghan might have taken the time to be fascinated by it if she wasn't melting into a warm fluid puddle and in danger of disappearing down the drain herself. He collapsed on top of her, forgetting for a moment to take some of the weight. They lay there in languid repletion for a few moments before Dean slipped out of her and rolled onto his side on the floor.

"God damn Meaghan you'll be the death of me," he said.

"The germs we're picking up on this floor will be the death of you," Meaghan countered, making Dean laugh tiredly before he sat up and attempted to help her up as well. He was surprisingly weak and clumsy but between them, they managed to get each other to their feet. They hosed themselves down again in the shower before taking the party to the bedroom where Meaghan flopped into bed naked.

"Hey, you wanna watch Fast 6 before we sleep?" Dean asked.

"We're running a bit behind if we're going to be up to date by the time Furious 7 comes out."

"Yeah, let's," Meaghan said jumping out of bed and grabbing Dean's robe. Dean held out his hand for her to take and they walked to the living room where Dean put the movie in and Meaghan foraged in the kitchen for snacks. She found some peanuts in one of the drawers as well as left over baked goods from breakfast...and some coffee.

Dean looked up as she came back into the room and made a face.

"Coffee? Really? There's plenty of booze," he said.

"Uh huh," she said putting down the cups of coffee on the table next to the muffins.

Dean rolled his eyes. "You're just too healthy for me."

"Coffee and baked goods at..." Meaghan glanced at the clock, "2 in the morning isn't exactly healthy," she protested.

"Yeah well my last girlfriend was inclined to try coke at this time," Dean said.

"Really?!?" Meaghan exclaimed. "And they say it's the poor black kids doing drugs," she murmured.

"Don't tell anyone," Dean said.

"Did you?" Meaghan asked curiously.

"Did I what?" Dean asked distractedly.

"Did you try the coke?" Meaghan spoke slowly as if he was mentally impaired.

Dean shook his head, "Nah, I had no desire to be thinner than I am. And I wasn't trying to run away from nothin' in my life."

"I thought you weren't happy with your life...before," Meaghan said.

"I wasn't…" Dean said thoughtfully. "Well I guess I'm just more well-adjusted emotionally," he continued breezily.

"Ha!" Meaghan said.

"What? You disagree?"

Meaghan shrugged, "Hey babe, I'm just here for the coffee and the movie."

"Really? And here I thought it was the sex," Dean said smiling.

"Shows how much *you* know," Meaghan replied drinking her coffee.

Dean's smile increased in wattage. "I love you kid."

"Ditto," Meaghan replied watching her movie.

Chapter 11

Bain took Meaghan shopping before their dinner date the following Thursday. The benefit was scheduled for the following Saturday and Meaghan hadn't yet had time to buy something suitable. Or rather she didn't have the motivation to go shopping alone; she wanted to go with Bain but didn't want to offend Dean. Thankfully Bain took the decision out of her hands by dragging her off to the Albright Fashion Library since she wouldn't allow him to buy her anything.

"Besides, it's not like I'll need it after today," she argued.

"Oh yeah? Will you be breaking up with Dean after the function or something?" Bain wanted to know.

"No but...even if he was to take me somewhere else, I can't really repeat the outfit right? So come on, take me to this rent place so I can get my designer duds on," she said.

They riffled through the selection of clothes, shoes, handbags and accessories with Bain saying if she was going to rent she might as well get an entire outfit. Meaghan had to be the voice of restraint if her credit card wasn't going to start loudly protesting her use of it.

"Dating a rich guy is so complicated," she complained to Bain.

"*Some* rich guys…others are pretty cool. Like me," Bain replied.

Meaghan rolled her eyes and went to try on the dresses Bain had picked out for her.

*****

Dr. Shelley was waiting for her when she came in to work the next morning, standing in front of her office with a smile on his face. In spite of the smile, Meaghan's stomach dropped in anxiety. Ever since the incident with Dean and her screaming in ecstasy for the whole corridor to hear, she'd been waiting for the other shoe to drop. She knew there'd been *some* talk but then Julie Anderson's son had been shot in the leg by a police officer's stray bullet and that had been the hot topic ever since. Julie was a regular client at the clinic and she'd brought her son in, bleeding and crying; scared out of his wits because he thought he was dying. He was still in the recovery ward, and garnering a lot of attention in the neighborhood. A local TV station had even done a feature on him.

She smiled back at Conrad as she opened her door and ushered him in. "What's up Conrad?" she asked trying not to show her nerves.

Conrad smiled at her. "Well it's been nine months since you joined us at the foundation and I just wanted to give you a bit of a score card."

Meaghan's heart descended to her toes, "Okay."

"I just want to say that in all the time I've been working in the medical field I have yet to meet more of a natural than you. It's not just medical knowledge; you know how to speak to the patients, their loved ones – you make them feel comfortable and cared for. You're thorough in your work; make sure that you do things right without wasting time. I gotta say Meaghan; sometimes I'm envious of your natural ability."

Meaghan was speechless.

"I...don't know what to say," she said.

Conrad smiled again. "No need to say anything. I just wanted you to know that you're doing a good job." He held out his hand for her to shake and she took it bemusedly then he left her to her work.

As soon as her legs could move again she fished out her phone and then hesitated. Her speed dial one was Bain, and her speed dial two was Dean (her mother was speed dial 0) and Mr Henley was four. The hospital rounded out the top five on her speed dial. She hesitated between 0, 1 and 2 wondering who she should call first. Or maybe a conference call? She shook her head and lowered her thumb, letting it fall where it would. She suppressed the sigh of relief she felt when it fell on 1. She'd really wanted to tell Bain but she knew that if her mother or Dean knew that they would be unhappy.

"Hey babe," Bain answered.

"Hey there," Meaghan said grinning brightly. "How is your morning going?"

"Never mind me, what's up?" Bain asked...and that was why he got the first phone call; he always knew when something was up.

"Well, Conrad Shelley just came by to give me an evaluation on my first nine months on the job," she said.

"And," Bain asked.

"He says I'm the most natural doctor he's ever seen," Meaghan said not even attempting to keep the smugness from her tone.

"Well I could have told you that," Bain said.

"Yes well you're biased," Meaghan said.

"So go on...tell me every word he said," Bain said. And that was the second reason he got the first phone call; he knew exactly what to say at all times. So Meaghan told him word for word what doctor

Shelley had said. He exclaimed in all the right places and was as excited as she was for each sentence that Conrad had uttered.

"That's really great, do you wanna go for lunch later and explore what it all means?" Bain asked. Meaghan opened her mouth to say yes but then thought that Dean might have the same idea and she didn't want to tell him – again – that she already had something set up with Bain so she said, "I'll check back with you later on that."

Bain was easy with that, as expected and she hung up and called her mother.

"Oh darling, that is so great. Though I'm not at all surprised; you were always very compassionate and also very careful with everything you did. It's natural that it would translate into your work. I'm just so happy it fulfills you."

Meaghan felt a lump in her throat at her mother's words. Bain might be good at saying all the expected things but her mother was the best at making her feel all soppy and emotional and like she needed to get home and give her a hug. She also missed her father abominably all of a sudden. She knew her mother was thinking of him too.

"Your father would have been so proud," she said right on cue. Having been a field medic in the American army fighting in Iraq, who'd been killed by friendly fire, this might very well be true. She was walking in his footsteps in a way, helping people who were in different kinds of trenches; surviving on the wicked streets of ghetto New York. Her mother too, as a nurse had carried on that fight. Meaghan was struck anew by the family legacy she was carrying on. What Dr. Shelley had said about her being an absolute natural seemed to take on greater significance and she fought not to let the tears fall.

"I love you mom," she said.

"I love you too. Shall I see you tonight?" she asked.

"Absolutely," Meaghan said. It was high time she and her mother spent some quality time. It had been a while.

She called Dean last after signing off with her mother while suppressing a twinge of guilt. Where did boyfriends rank in the space-time continuum as pertained to levels of importance in one's life? He answered right away.

"Hallo Meaghan," he said very formally and she knew he was not alone. She looked at her office clock; it was 9 am in the morning which meant that he might be at work. Perhaps he was with his secretary.

"Hi. Can you talk right now?" she asked.

"Er, I actually have a meeting but can I call you back?" he asked.

"Yeah okay," Meaghan said stretching her mouth in a smile as if he could see her.

"Okay," Dean said and then there was an awkward silence.

"Yeah so bye," Meaghan said.

"Talk to you later Meaghan," he replied and hung up.

Meaghan leaned back in her chair and sighed; well...that was why he was last. She turned to her work files, picking up the first one and studying the patient history.

She was hard at work, dealing with the distraught mother of a young boy who had just been diagnosed with Hodgkin's lymphoma when she glanced to the side after catching sight of a familiar profile. A tall man wearing an expensive gray suit was strolling down the corridor toward her. He drew the eye of every red-blooded female that he passed, maybe a few of the males too. Meaghan stopped talking abruptly and even the distressed woman she was speaking to looked up briefly. Meaghan turned back to her and led her gently back to the waiting room. Her son was undergoing tests to measure exactly how extensive the cancer was and it would take a while. Meaghan called for an orderly to get the mother some coffee and then pressed some pamphlets into her hands so she could educate herself.

"Do you have someone you can call to come wait with you?" she asked.

The mother shook her head sadly. "It's just me and Jeremy," she said.

Meaghan squeezed her hand then straightened up turning to the shadow she could see on her right.

"Hey," Dean said quietly, hands in his pockets.

"Dean," she replied and moved to go past him, leading the way to her office.

"Janice," she told the receptionist, "Five minutes break before the next patient?"

Janice nodded agreeably. Was there a knowing look in her eyes? Meaghan couldn't quite tell. Dean was more or less a fixture in her life these days but he didn't usually drop in in the middle of the day.

"What's up?" she asked as soon as the door to her office was closed behind her.

"This is me returning your call," he said smiling.

Meaghan stared in stupefaction. "Really? Because I'm pretty sure our phone signal still works."

Dean laughed. "Yeah I know but you sounded like you wanted to tell me something important and were disappointed that I couldn't talk so I wanted to come down and look you in the eyes as you told me...whatever it is."

Meaghan continued to stare. "You're serious?" she said incredulously.

"Yes I'm serious. Okay and I had a site meeting not far from here so I thought I'd take a detour," he continued.

"Ah. That makes it all far less disturbing," Meaghan said.

"So? What did you want to tell me?" he asked.

Meaghan opened her mouth and then closed it again. Now that he'd come all this way, she felt like she should maybe have something much more significant to tell him about than some positive evaluation. She felt quite awkward in fact and braced herself for his disappointment.

"Well you see, this morning Conrad Shelley came to see me," she began.

"Oh? What did he want?"Dean asked all hostile vigilance and Meaghan remembered that he did not like her boss for simply being potential competition, which he would never be in a million years but Dean couldn't seem to get that.

"He wanted to give me an evaluation of my performance since I started working at the foundation," she said looking at his lapel rather than into his deep green eyes.

Dean leaned back on her table one leg bent and the other stretched to balance his weight. "And?" he asked sounding like he was ready to explode if Dr. Shelley had said one wrong word to her.

Meaghan told him everything Dr. Shelley had said. He listened silently, intent green eyes trained on her face, taking in not just what she was saying with her mouth but also her body. When she finished he reached out and took her hand in his.

"What can I say? It sounds like it's everything you ever dreamed," he said.

"It is and yet it's something I never expected," she said eyes shining. He was watching her intently as if taking in every single particle of her being. "All I ever hoped for, dreamed of; is being a surgeon. If I was lucky, I would be a good one; a successful one. But to have this doctor that I respect so much tell me that I'm the most natural doctor he's ever seen..." Meaghan shook her head, lost for words.

Dean squeezed her hand smiling into her eyes, "It's vindication."

"Yes...vindication, validation...it's...everything," she told him.

He smiled at her and nodded, "I get it."

"You do?" she asked searching his eyes for any hint of prevarication or pandering.

"I do," he said.

Meaghan smiled as she remembered why she loved him so much, and why he was even a factor on her space-time continuum.

"I love you so much," she said.

Dean smiled at her, "and there is *my* vindication; *my* validation."

Meaghan pushed him lightly on the chest. "You're such a sap," she said with a side smile. "Now go get to your meeting."

"Yes ma'am," Dean said leaning forward a little bit to meet her lips.

"You want to have lunch with me? Celebrate?" she asked him suddenly.

Dean smiled, "I'd love to. Pick you up at one?"

"Yes please," Meaghan said stepping back out of the way so he could pass.

"See you then," he said opening the door to her office.

"Bye," she called and looked at her watch. They'd been in her office eight minutes. She leaned out to catch Janice's eye so as to let her know she could send in the next patient. As she was waiting for them to come in she quickly texted Bain to tell him that lunch was a rain check.

*****

The site meeting was actually at Hallets Point with Bain and Conrad Shelley. It was the potential site for a recreation center that the

Wesson Foundation was interested in building for Dr. Shelley's Queens Foundation. After hearing Meaghan go on and on for months about the work that they did and the people that they helped and keeping in mind that his foundation was on the hunt for a new project to support; it had seemed like the perfect marriage. However he hadn't wanted to tell Meaghan about it because he didn't want to be the boyfriend who threw money around in an attempt to impress his girl and maybe, she might think he was trying to buy her way into a promotion or whatever it was doctors got. And he didn't want anyone else to think that Meaghan had tried to strong arm him into doing this for her own benefit. He really hoped that this project wasn't the reason why Meaghan had got a good review from Conrad. He did mean to ask him about it though. If he was being totally honest, one of the reasons he'd chosen Dr. Shelley's foundation was to keep an eye on the man. Not that he would admit that even under pain of death. It was his dirty little secret.

Bain was the architect on the project because Conrad had met him at *La Trattoria* with Meaghan at one of their ubiquitous dates there. They'd hit it off and when this project was proposed, Conrad had said he knew just the architect to take it up. It helped that Bain was willing to work at cost but Dean still didn't have to like it. Still, they managed to keep a civil tongue in their heads for these meetings and things were going smoothly. Surprisingly Bain had honored his request not to tell Meaghan about the project *just yet*. He had a feeling it was because of some simpering romantic notion of his but Dean was not about to complain.

Bain was already at the site when Dean arrived, hard hat in place as he had an animated conversation with the foreman. Dean stepped out of his car and walked toward them, meeting Conrad midway as he came out of the makeshift office with a hardhat and a second one slung across his arm. He handed this one to Dean with a smile of greeting and they both went up to see what the issue was that

Bain and the foreman were discussing with such energy.

*****

Meaghan took the train home that evening after having to actively

dissuade Dean from coming over to pick her up. She reminded him

that they had a date with a museum the following evening and

therefore he should take the out she was giving him and go do

something fun. She passed through Mr. Henley's garage just to say

hello and remind herself again of the good ol' days when she used

to do his accounts for five dollars an hour. He tended to also count

the hours when she was just hanging out in his office reading a

book or doing homework so it racked up to quite a bit of time. Mr.

Henley was lounging outside his garage leaning against the wall.

Meaghan wanted to chide him on how smoking was really bad for

his diabetes but refrained. After all, he'd managed to live this long without her monitoring his health for him so she wasn't going to start now.

"Hi Mr. Henley," she called.

"Oh hi Ms. Sunshine. Have you come to help me with the books today?" he asked smiling through the smoke.

"You want me to look through the books for ya?" she asked.

"If you have the time," Mr. Henley said.

"I always have time for you Mr. Henley," Meaghan said.

"Wonderful. Come by later after your mom has gone to bed. I acquired something you'll be jazzed to see," he said looking pleased with himself.

"Which album?" she asked stopping to lean on the wall next to him.

He looked at her with a twinkle in his eye, acknowledging that she'd got it in one guess. "AC/DC, Back in Black. First edition."

"Seriously?" she exclaimed in excitement.

"Seriously," Mr. Henley confirmed nodding his head.

"Tell you what, I'll do your books for you if you play it for me while I work," she said.

"Deal," he agreed holding out his hand to be shook.

Meaghan went off to her house to see her mother, looking forward to dinner. Her mother could *cook*. Amanda Leonard was waiting for her as she came through the door.

"Meaghan? Is that you?" she called from the kitchen and Meaghan hurried in that direction pulled by the delicious smells emanating from there.

"Hey mom," she called as she hurried.

Amanda turned to look at her with a delighted smile as she walked in.

"Well look whose here," she said.

Meaghan spread her hands out. "Ta da! Mommy I'm home," she sing songed.

Amanda opened her arms and Meaghan came into them.

"I feel like I haven't seen you for three years," Amanda said.

"I know mom, I've been MIA what with the job and the boyfriend... I'm sorry."

"Don't be sorry. You're supposed to leave your parents behind," Amanda said.

"Never," Meaghan replied vehemently. Amanda chuckled and went back to her stirring and Meaghan pulled out a chair to update her on everything in her life.

*****

After dinner she went over to the shop to visit with Mr. Henley and do his books. The garage bay was full of muscle cars and 'Back in Black' was blasting from the speakers. Meaghan walked in with a smile and greeted the various mechanics as she passed. A group of

beat boys were clustered near one of the cars, talking and laughing

loudly and drinking beers. Sometimes it happened that

neighborhood boys would use the garage as a hang out. They

thought it was cool and Mr. Henley wasn't averse as long as they

didn't cause any trouble.

She took the stairs up to the office and knocked slowly. She could

hear voices inside and wondered if maybe Mr. Henley was dealing

with a client.

"Come in," he called in his hoarse voice, affected by all the nicotine

he'd consumed over the years.

She opened the door ready with her professional smile and it

dropped off her face when she saw who was in the office with Mr.

Henley.

"Dean," she said in surprise.

"Hey Meaghan," he replied.

Chapter 12

"What are you doing here?" Meaghan asked Dean who was sitting at Mr. Henley's desk with his feet up.

"I called Jefferson here and he told me that you might be coming by later and that I was welcome to come by and wait," Dean said.

Meaghan almost asked who Jefferson was but realized in time that Mr. Henley's first name couldn't be Mr.

"Oh, so you came to hang out at a garage I may or may not have come to just on the off chance?" she asked Dean.

"There really was very little risk that you wouldn't come. After all you promised Jefferson right?" he said.

"Mr. Henley. I promised Mr. Henley," she replied supremely uncomfortable with the familiarity. Her mother had always emphasized respect for older folk and that included not calling them by their first names as if they were age mates. Mr. Henley had always been old to her, even when she was very young.

"Anyway, the point is moot because here you are," Mr. Henley said standing up. He pointed toward a pile of books.

"There is your work, waiting for you and if you perk your ears up you will hear the sounds of For Those About to Rock blasting through the speakers. Very apropos don't you think?" he said.

Meaghan saluted him and he smiled back and then left the office to them.

"Wow, you really can't resist me huh?" she teased.

"I can resist you; I just don't want to," Dean replied smiling. He picked up one of the accounting ledgers and leafed through it.

"Hey! I'm supposed to do the books not you," she protested pulling it out of his hands.

Dean shrugged. "Okay but I just thought it'd go faster if we helped each other. Jefferson is cool with it if that's what's bothering you,"

"Okay then," Meaghan said tossing him the first ledger. She was doing her best not to grin like an idiot at the fact that Dean came to hang out with Mr. Henley so he could see her tonight...despite the fact that they would see each other tomorrow.

"How is your dad doing?" she asked.

"He's taking to the robotics really well," Dean said with a smile. "He's able to feed himself now and articulate his needs. You can really see how much happier he is."

"That is wonderful," Meaghan said.

"You should come visit him sometime, I'm sure he'd like to express his gratitude to you personally," he suggested.

Meaghan shook her head. "I didn't do anything but suggest an idea. It was his doctors who did the rest."

"Yeah, after you put us in touch with the right ones. Come on Megs, take the credit where the credit is due," Dean said.

"The amount of backlash that got me though...I hardly like to think about it," Meaghan said.

"That lawsuit was bogus," Dean scoffed. "There is no way the Medical Board or a court of law could have taken it seriously. And my father's doctors wouldn't even have filed if my mother hadn't been on their asses about it."

"Another thing I don't like to think about..."Meaghan said wryly.

Dean leaned forward and covered her hand with his. "This too shall pass," he said with a small smile. Meaghan made a non-committal sound and went back to her books.

*****

They were still asleep when Meaghan's phone went off. They were sleeping in; it was Saturday morning and they were both without commitments for the morning. Meaghan reached sleepily forward groping at the bedside table without opening her eyes. She grasped it and brought it to her ear, making an incoherent grunting sound that the caller could take as he would.

"Babe, are you coming over here so I can get you ready for the ball or what?" Bain asked.

"What are you my fairy godmother now?" Meaghan replied grumpily.

"I thought we'd established that over ten years ago. Now when are you getting here?" he asked.

"I don't know. Late afternoon probably?" Meaghan said.

Bain made a dissenting sound, "that's cutting it pretty fine. We might not be able to work in a full facial with that time frame."

"Are there half-facials?" Meaghan wanted to know still with eyes closed.

"Not for us darling. Make it early afternoon okay? So go have sex with that boyfriend of yours now so you can get away in time," he replied and hung up.

Meaghan giggled, dropped her phone on the night stand, swept the covers over her head, turned around and went back to sleep. She could feel Dean curling into himself in front of her and placed her hand gently on his back as she drifted off to sleep again. He leaned into her hand but didn't wake, snoring away contentedly.

It was the baked goods delivery guy that woke them finally. Carmen did not come in on Saturdays so there was no-one to get the door but one of them. Dean ignored the doorbell but Meaghan couldn't. She fished out his house coat and ventured downstairs to answer the door. The delivery guy greeted her familiarly – she was a well-known face by now – and handed her the breakfast basket before taking off. She took it upstairs and put the coffee on, quite at home by this time in his kitchen to not hesitate over using his stuff. She made herself some coffee and then retired to his tiny patio with a muffin and the day's paper.

"So boogie of you Leonard," she murmured to herself as she settled in the wicker chair with her coffee, crossing her legs as she scanned the paper for news. It was the same old, same old as far as she could tell so she turned to the comics section to get her hit of Boondocks and Marmaduke – a much better way to start the day in her opinion than all the bad news and negativity.

She was just settling down, feet up on the guard rail and about to start in on her coffee when Dean ambled over, kissing her absently on the forehead before going off to get his own cup of coffee.

"Morning," he mumbled as he came back, flopped down on the other wicker chair and gestured for her to hand over the sports pages. Dean was not a morning person.

"G'mornin," she replied with a small smile.

"How'd you sleep?" he asked.

"Like a drunk baby," she said grinning at him. He smiled back at her, leaned back and drank his coffee as he scanned the pages of the New York Times.

"How would a drunk baby sleep anyway?" Dean mused. "Wouldn't they be like, in danger of dying?"

"Convulsions, drowning in their own vomit, CNS depression – it's not just babies though...anyone could suffer any of those." Meaghan informed him.

"Good to know," he said with irony standing up to go get another cup. He'd inhaled the first one as if it was a glass of cool water. Dean was like that with coffee. It was his drug of choice.

"Bain tells me I have to leave here by early afternoon if he's to turn me into Cinderella in time for the ball," Meaghan said and Dean grimaced. He always grimaced when Bain was mentioned.

"He knows that you're going with *me* right?" Dean said. Meaghan laughed in resignation.

"He's just trying to make me all pretty for you," Meaghan said.

"You're already pretty for me," Dean protested.

"Aww, I'd say you're so sweet if I didn't know where that compliment was coming from."

"What do you mean?" Dean asked.

"Don't be obtuse," Meaghan replied.

Dean was silent, polishing off his muffin. "I do think you're going to be the most beautiful thing at this ball. Right now, in this moment, before Bain has laid a hand on you or you've put on your finery."

"Thank you Dean, you say the nicest things," Meaghan replied impassively but she was smiling impishly and giving him side long glances as she did so.

Dean glanced at her as if to gauge her words and then went back to his newspaper. They read in silence for the rest of the meal.

*****

It was a full house; Daniel had taken the day off from work, Bain's phone was off and even Bella was invited for the beauty primping session. Or rather she'd asked to join in. Meaghan wondered why, considering that she had friends who were going to this shindig that she could prepare with.

"I don't know, you guys seem like a lot of fun," she'd said with a shrug when Meaghan asked. Meaghan decided to shrug it off too and take it all in stride. What's the worst that could happen after all?

Mei and her colleagues all converged at Bain's house with every implement known to man or woman to enhance their beauty. They began with full body massages followed by combination facial/mani-pedi. A specialist was brought in for Meaghan's hair, the Asians not knowing exactly how to style it. After hair was make up and then the beauticians left so that they could prepare their outfits. It was just going on 7pm by then and Meaghan was expecting Dean to pick her up by eight. She wouldn't have thought it would take the full hour to put on a dress and some shoes but somehow when Dean drew up at the house, she wasn't ready yet. At least not to Bain's satisfaction.

She had selected elegant couture dark purple one shoulder evening dress made from imitated silk with kitted lining and beaded embroidery. She paired with six inch strapless sandals made of pink velvet and a black Chanel handbag. Dean walked into the room and stopped short as if he'd hit an invisible barrier. His mouth opened but nothing came out for several minutes.

"I stand corrected," he said looking her up and down. She was checking him out too; his tall elegant form was encased in a black tuxedo which fit him like a glove. His blinding white shirt contrasted nicely with his velvet black bow tie. The result was James Bond in his prime, a glittering Adonis that was blinding to behold.

"Wow," Meaghan said checking him out. "You look…"

"So do you," he replied. It was like there was no-one else in the room for a moment.

Meaghan shook her head as if waking from a doze. "What do you stand corrected about?"

"That you could possibly look better? Did I say better? Not the right word. But you're dazzling," he said.

Meaghan laughed, "I get it. I clean up pretty good," she said smugly.

"That you do," Dean agreed. He held out his arm to her.

"Shall we go?" he asked. Meaghan started, she wanted to ask about waiting for Bain and Daniel but she knew what the answer would be so she just hastened forward to take his arm. He smiled at her and then looked up at Bain lounging in the entrance to the hallway. He lifted his hand in salute and actually smiled at him. Meaghan took that as a positive thing and then they left.

"I thought we'd have dinner first," Dean said as they were driving. "The food at these events can be a bit dodgy."

"Okay," Meaghan agreed.

"Can you eat in that dress?" Dean asked.

Meaghan looked down at herself; sure her dress was defining of her figure, hugging her all the way down to her hips before flaring out in asymmetrical elegance still...it wasn't like she was wearing a corset or whatever.

"Why couldn't I eat?" she ventured.

Dean shrugged and smiled, eyes on the road. "I love that you even ask that."

Meaghan looked at him with a quizzical smile, waiting for an explanation. Dean shrugged again, "Samantha wouldn't eat like for two days if she had to attend such functions."

www.SaucyRomanceBooks.com/RomanceBooks

Meaghan snorted derisively but didn't say anything. Dean glanced at her, waiting for her to elaborate on the sound she'd made but she just continued to look out the window at the passing scenery. Her hair blew about her face in curling ringlets, and there was a diamond pin in the form of a flower pinned on one side of her hair as if it *was* a flower.

"Where'd you get the jewelry?" Inquiring minds wanted to know.

Meaghan turned away from the window to look at Dean, "I rented it."

Dean's eyebrows quirked and he nodded. "I should have got you some jewelry long ago," he chided himself.

"What? Got me jewelry from where?" she asked genuinely puzzled.

"Oh you know, how when you have a boyfriend he buys you jewelry? Especially if he's done something wrong, you've had a fight, it's the anniversary of the day you first bumped into each other...that kind of shit?" Dean said.

Meaghan laughed, "Really?"

"Really," Dean replied. "Anyway, I've clearly been remiss so I'll get right on that."

Meaghan laughed again shaking her head, "You're crazy."

"*You're* crazy," Dean replied as he turned in at a restaurant. He alighted at the entrance and took her hand. It seemed like the restaurant was expecting them because they were led right to a table in a secluded corner. There was already wine cooling in an ice bucket and rolls in a basket. Meaghan picked one up as the waiter placed menus in their hands.

"I'll have the fish," Meaghan said handing the menu to the waiter. "Fish and potatoes with a side of greens please."

"I'll have the same," Dean said handing his menu back as well. They studied each other as they waited for the food not saying anything. Dean smiled.

"Are you nervous?" he asked her.

"Yes," Meaghan replied at once.

Dean laughed. "You're supposed to protest; you're supposed to say nah, I'm fine, don't worry about me," Dean had made his voice higher and said it in a sing song voice.

"Have you ever known me to talk like that?" Meaghan asked looking offended.

Dean looked like he was thinking about it, "Not that I can recall but anyway I wasn't imitating you I was just…"

"Making fun of me," Meaghan finished for him.

"Right," he agreed.

"Okay then so back to the fact that I'm nervous, any wise words for me?" Meaghan asked.

"Yes. Just remember what a great person you are and walk in there with supreme confidence. The rest will follow."

"Wow. Actual wise words," Meaghan said wryly with an eye roll.

"I *can* step up on occasion," Dean said self-deprecatingly.

"Good to know."

Dean covered her hand with his. "Seriously though, you have nothing to worry about. Everyone will love you."

"Everyone who doesn't already hate my guts you mean," she qualified.

"No, I mean everyone," Dean said.

"Is your mother going to be in attendance?" Meaghan asked and Dean had the grace to grimace.

"She might drop in," he said.

"And Samantha?" Meaghan asked next, though she tried to avoid saying that name if she could.

Dean shrugged, "I have no knowledge of Samantha's schedule so I actually have no idea."

"Really? None of your so-called friends have given you the heads up on that?" she pressed.

"Nope," Dean said.

"And you-"

"Look. Meaghan. We can spend our whole lives worrying about running into Samantha or whatever, or we can just live. I vote for the latter," Dean interrupted.

Meaghan smiled and nodded, "You're probably right,"

"I *am* right," Dean said.

They finished their dinner and then headed to the museum.

*****

Poppy walked into Jeffrey's room to show him her dress for the ball. It was a yellow confection that on someone else might have looked too young, but on her it fit like it was made for her. Which, of course, it was. She did a slow pirouette so Jeffrey could see her from all angles and he smiled his delight at her. He didn't have to say he thought she was beautiful; she could see it in his eyes. She took a seat on his bed and leaned into him resting her coiffed head on his and bumping their shoulders together.

"I don't know what to do with him Jeff; he's making this huge mistake and every time I try to help him he pushes me further and further away," she said to him softly. His hand rose slowly and moved to cover hers.

"This woman is no good for him, why can't he see that?" she asked him plaintively.

"You can't tell him⋯what to do" the computer intoned.

Poppy sighed. "I miss the days when I could," she moaned and felt Jeffrey shake with laughter. "She's going to be there you know? Dean is bringing her with him," she continued quietly. He squeezed her hand.

www.SaucyRomanceBooks.com/RomanceBooks

"Oh don't worry, I won't make a scene. It just hurts my heart to have to be civil to this gold digger person. And that's what she is you know?" she said sitting up and fixing Jeffrey with a glare. He looked back at her, a wry look in his eye and quirked his brow; much like his son was fond of doing.

"I need a drink," Poppy said sitting up and ringing the bell next to the bed. Reeves appeared not long after and she ordered a glass of champagne to be brought to her.

"Would you like a glass Jeffrey?" she asked him. He smiled at her in amusement and shook his head slightly. He was on several different medications and they did not mix well with alcohol. Still he appreciated the thought. Reeves brought a flute of perfectly chilled Brut for her and she downed it before standing up and smoothing down her dress.

"Do I look presentable?" she asked him moving her hips from side to side so he could properly see how lovingly the dress draped over her still shapely curves.

"Beautiful" the computer announced in that robotic tone that stripped the words of their emotion. Nevertheless Poppy could see Jeffrey's face and that was all she needed to understand every single emotion behind the word.

"I'll see you later," she said softly and swept out of the room. Jeffrey followed her with his eyes and his ears until he couldn't hear the click clack of her heels descending the stairs anymore.

*****

They drew up at the museum, designed by Frank Lloyd Wright with an architecturally significant spiral rotunda. The driveway was already full of cars and the whole place was gaily lit up. A butler looking individual was waiting at the door to take their coats and usher them into the restaurant that was set up for the function.

Another usher was on hand to receive them and lead them to their seats, which were definitely at the VIP table if Meaghan knew anything about such things. A number of older white gentlemen and ladies were sitting at the table already. Dean smiled and greeted them by name, evidently he knew them all, and then turned to introduce her. She took her cue from him and smiled as well, shaking hands and acting like she was used to conversing with people wearing millions in jewelry all the time. Dean told her a bit about every person she was introduced to; hedge fund managers and company CEOs, founders, owners, the odd celebrity as well. Meaghan smiled and smiled while her stomach roiled and the fish she'd eaten sat uneasily in it. Still she found that Dean's advice was good and acting like she belonged made everyone treat her like she did.

That was until the formalities were completed, insane amounts of money had been pledged and the floor was open for dancing...

Chapter 13

Meaghan was in the powder room, touching up her make up when two blonde heads appeared on either side of her. She looked from one to the other; since she grew up on the street her radar for trouble was in perfect working order. And this? This was trouble.

They were staring at her in the mirror as they touched up their lipstick, crowding her in a way that was subtle yet uncompromising. The fat lady wiping her hands on the other side of the room left and then there were three.

"So you seem to have Dean Wesson wrapped around your little finger huh," Blonde on the Left said.

Meaghan straightened up. "Who are you?" she asked furrowing her brow in puzzlement like she was trying to place her. Which she wasn't. She knew she'd never seen them before in her life, but also that they were some of Samantha's ubiquitous friends.

"Wrong question," Blonde on the right said, her eyes shooting lasers at Meaghan if only this was a star wars movie. "The question you should be asking is 'what is going to happen to me now?'" she continued.

"Oh...you're badass now huh? What, you gonna administer a beat down on me? You all gangsta up in here in your designer threads?" Meaghan said derisively.

Both blondes glared. "You're a crazy trashy gold digger who has no right-" Blonde on the left said glaring at her.

"No right? And here I thought it was a free country," Meaghan sneered.

"Dean will find out who you are sooner or later. Then he'll drop you like the rubbish you are," Blonde on the right said.

"I guess we'll just have to wait and see won't we," Meaghan said snatching up her rented bag and sweeping elegantly out of the room. The two blondes watch her go with identical glares on their faces.

Meaghan took a deep fortifying breath as soon as she was out of the room and went in search of Bain. She'd spotted him and Daniel last at the bar so that's the direction she went. She needed her friend right now.

She spotted Daniel first, getting drinks from one of the bartenders and followed him back to the table where Bain was sitting, conversing with Poppy Wesson of all people. Meaghan almost turned away but Bain spotted her and waved her over.

"Shit," she murmured and walked slowly toward them searching with her peripheral vision to see if she could spot Dean anywhere. He'd been waltzing with a lovely old lady with long waves of butter white hair when she'd gone to the ladies. Shouldn't be too hard to spot. But she couldn't see anyone.

"Bain," she said as she walked up to the table, the strain in her voice obvious even to her. She darted a glance at Poppy and smiled slightly. "Mrs. Wesson," she said.

Bain reached out a hand to her and pulled her into the empty seat next to him as Daniel darted her a sympathetic glance from across the table and Poppy acted like she didn't exist.

"I was just telling Poppy about your wonderful project that you run in Queens helping inner city children," Bain said.

"Well I don't exactly run it; I just work there," Meaghan qualified.

"She's so modest," Bain cut in even before she'd finished the sentence. "So selfless and loving. The kids love her," he continued and Meaghan felt her face heat up. Whatever Bain thought he was doing, she appreciated it but she wished he would stop.

Meaghan cleared her throat and looked significantly at him but he ignored her.

"The whole thing is ran by Dr. Conrad Shelley; you've heard of him right?" Bain said to Poppy who was trying her best to look forbidding yet polite at the same time. Meaghan was fascinated to see that she was pulling it off quite nicely.

"Conrad Shelley?" she repeated suddenly coming to life.

"Yes, you know him right?" Bain said radiating satisfaction.

"He is a doctor of good repute," she conceded.

"*Adores* Meaghan," Bain said, drawing out the first word as he placed his hand on Poppy's arm rather familiarly Meaghan thought. Considering how much he and Dean did not get along, she didn't imagine he'd had the chance to get that close to Poppy.

"Bainbury," Poppy said and there was warning in her tone that he might just be going too far.

"Oh come on Poppy, bend a little," Bain said and Meaghan's heart almost stopped. *What was he doing?*

www.SaucyRomanceBooks.com/RomanceBooks

"I should get back to my table. Please remind your mother about tea on Saturday," Poppy said standing up.

"Will do," Bain said quietly and she walked away. Meaghan hit him on the arm immediately.

"What was that?" she demanded of him.

"I was just trying to talk you up," Bain protested and Daniel snorted a laugh. Both of them turned to glare at him and he put his hands up in surrender.

"I didn't even know you knew Poppy like that," Meaghan said with a furrow of her brow.

"Our mothers are in the DAR together. Dean and I kind of had to tolerate each other from a very early age," Bain said grudgingly.

"Well….I'm glad your mutual antagonism isn't all on my account. But seriously Bain, what was that?" Meaghan said refusing to be sidetracked.

"Look, Poppy came over here to ask me to speak to you about leaving her son alone because she'd heard we were friends. I, in turn, countered with how about she gave you a chance to show you how awesome you are? That's when you came over," Bain said.

Meaghan's heart had dropped right into her shoes; some days, like this one, she despaired of ever getting through to Dean's mother. And if she couldn't do that then...

"Hey, don't look like that," Daniel said reaching across the table for her hand. He was dressed all in white, his suit was terribly fitting; it hugged him everywhere and put every inch of his marvelous body on display. Nevertheless it was tastefully made and clearly expensive, and Daniel was a god; so he got away with it. Meaghan tried to smile at him, watching his blonde hair glinting in the light from the overhead lamps but didn't quite manage it.

"Meaghan! Fancy meeting you here," a male voice said from behind her and she metaphorically girded her loins to deal with this new threat. She turned around not knowing what to expect, to see Conrad Shelley smiling down at her. He had a buxom red head on his arm; she looked kind of bored but determined to see this through. Meaghan envied her, her motivation – whatever it was.

"Conrad! This is a surprise," she said standing up to greet him. He gave her the up and down look and smiled.

"You clean up good," he said and she smiled.

"Thanks. You too." His black and white suit did indeed look extremely good on his six foot one athletic frame. The white side burns in his jet black hair added an air of sophistication that was sure to turn every head in the room. Meaghan wondered how it was that she was *surrounded* by all these good looking men.

"I didn't know you ran in these circles," he said inclining his head in inquiry.

"Dean," she said in explanation.

"Ah, the boyfriend. Where is he?" Conrad asked.

Meaghan looked around wondering the same thing herself but shrugged her shoulders at Conrad. "I have no idea," she said. Conrad turned to greet Bain and Daniel seemingly more familiar with them than Meaghan realized.

"I didn't know you'd met Daniel," she said to him.

"Oh he came down to the site with Bain one time while we were there. He brought sandwiches that he'd made. They were delicious," Conrad informed her with a smile.

"Site?" Meaghan asked curiously.

"Yeah you know, the site for the recreation center your boyfriend's foundation is building for us silly," Conrad said clearly expecting that Meaghan knew exactly what he was talking about. She raised her eyebrows so high they were almost touching her hair.

www.SaucyRomanceBooks.com/RomanceBooks

"My boyfriend what?" she asked and then Bain pulled her aside, suddenly claiming that he needed her to remove something from his eye...urgently.

"Dean is funding the recreation center y'all are building on Hallet's Point. We'll talk about it tomorrow," he whispered and then she blew enthusiastically into his eye for effect and they went back to the conversation with Conrad.

The band began a new song, an upbeat samba beat and Conrad asked her if she'd like to dance.

"Sure. Dancing with one's boss; not awkward at all," she murmured. Conrad laughed and swept her into his arm, leading her onto the dance floor while doing the steps. She couldn't help smiling her enjoyment and tossed all her worries away as she enjoyed the music.

*****

"Why is that man dancing with my girlfriend?" Dean said and was surprised when Daniel answered him. He hadn't been aware he was speaking out loud.

"Oh Dean lighten up; he's her boss and it's always a good thing to be friendly with your boss," Daniel said.

Dean turned to look at him. "Are *you* friendly with *your* boss?" he asked snarkily.

"I'm an independent contractor," Daniel said impassively.

"Oh right", Dean said nodding. "So really, why are they dancing?"

Meaghan and Conrad were cutting a swath across the dance floor. Her flowered purple dress was perfect for this dance; she seemed to have been born to dance the Samba. She and Conrad looked like they were in perfect sync as he tossed her this way and that, bending her over his arm in the classic pose. For one horrified second Dean was afraid he was going to kiss her. But he just flipped her back up and twirled her around as she laughed delightedly.

Dean took a step toward them even before he was aware he'd decided to cut in but Daniel's hand closed tightly on his arm.

"It's just a dance Dean," he said. "Let's not make it more than that."

Dean continued to glare at the couple.

"Hey Dean, meet Daneel; she's Conrad's date," Daniel said tugging him around to introduce him to a buxom red head standing nearby. She turned to greet him with a shy smile and then looked back at the dance floor. They were not the only ones watching the dancing couple. At least half the room had an eye on them.

"Your so-called girlfriend is making a spectacle of herself," a smug voice said from his other side as Samantha slipped into the spot next to him. He ignored her but she continued to speak to him.

"I really seriously don't know what you see in that attention whore. Obviously she'll slut it out for anyone who'll give her a leg up," she said. Dean wanted to reach a hand out and sock her in the jaw. Instead he ground his teeth and moved to the other side of the table putting Daniel between them. Bain stood up from where he was sitting and went to stand beside Samantha.

"Can I help you with something?" he asked her. She sneered at him.

"Oh look who it is; the attention whore's fag pimp", she said.

Bain smiled. "Happy now? Or haven't you used up your quota of offensive words yet?"

Samantha glared at him and then stalked off leaving the three men with the unwelcome feeling of presenting a united front.

Unwelcome at least for Dean and Bain. Daniel liked everybody.

The dance came to an end. Spontaneous applause from the watching crowd for Conrad and Meaghan and they took a bow before heading back to Bain's table. Meaghan was smiling at Dean, glad to have located him at last and Conrad was watching her smile at him with a slight furrow to his brow but a smile playing around his lips as well.

"Hey you," Meaghan said coming up to Dean and taking his hands delightedly.

"Hey," Dean replied pulling her until she was flush against him. "I didn't know you could samba like that."

"Viva Brazil," she said grinning at him. "Where were you? I couldn't find you anywhere."

"Is that why you decided to ditch me for the doc there?"

"Nah, that was actually to distract me from the mean girls I met in the ladies' followed by the impromptu mediation session Bain tried to hold with your mother right after."

"What?" Dean asked in puzzlement.

"Long story. Tell you later?" she said.

"Okay," Dean said holding her even closer if that was possible.

"And then you can tell me all about this project for Conrad's foundation that you're funding."

Dean stiffened. "Who told you?" he asked shooting a glare at Bain.

"Conrad. He seemed to be under the impression that I already knew," Meaghan said. Suddenly *she* stiffened and moved away from him. "Wait. Is that why he gave me that evaluation?" she asked staring suspiciously at him.

Dean sighed. "Megs…really? You really think I would do that?"

Meaghan stared at him a bit more. "I…guess not," she said quietly though she didn't sound a hundred per cent sure.

"I wouldn't," he clarified forcefully.

"Then why keep the project a secret?" she asked.

"Can we talk about this later?" he asked trying to pull her nearer again.

Meaghan studied him. "Sure but at this rate we're going to have to make a to-do list of Things to Discuss Later."

Dean smiled. "I'll get right on that," he said and then his face got serious. "I promise Megs as soon as we get home, we'll talk about this. This just isn't the right time or place."

"Okay," Meaghan said moving back into his arms. She was perturbed by all this secrecy but acknowledged that now wasn't the time to hash it out.

"My mother didn't say anything to you, did she?" he asked her.

"Nah. Bain was too busy talking me up for her to get a word in edgewise. I got the feeling she would have liked to though," she said.

"That's too bad. I was hoping she was coming around. She's been much happier since the whole improved ability to converse with dad now. In spite of the fact that it was your idea."

Meaghan smiled. "Let's not push it too hard. Whatever is going on with her, she needs to work it out for herself."

Dean looked down at her and smiled. "Do you want to dance?" he asked.

"Thought you'd never ask," Meaghan replied.

*****

Adriana sat by Jan feeling a little disappointed in how the evening had turned out. Rumor had it that Dean Wesson was single and she'd been hoping to take their budding business relationship to a whole other personal level starting with the killer red dress she was wearing tonight that outlined her every curve and caused her dusky complexion to shine. Her long legs encased in black Jimmy Choos with the red bottoms were the most 'fuck-me' shoes she'd ever seen but Dean had hardly spared her so much as a glance. All of his attention was for the purple clad black woman he'd come with. She was shorter than Adriana though not by much and her body was curvier but in the looks stakes, Adriana would definitely bet on herself being hotter than that nappy haired dark skinned...girl. Sure her skin was clear and unblemished and she had some real moves on the dance floor. She knew how to move her body to definite advantage and even Adriana could admit that ass she had on her was just perfect.

Still, all things considered, Adriana did not understand what it was that this woman had that she didn't. She sauntered casually up to the blonde that she'd seen the girl exchanging words with earlier and smiled at her, holding out her hand to be shook.

"Adriana Stuijt," she said cordially.

"Samantha Crawford," the blonde replied shaking her hand a bit grumpily.

"Would you mind if I ask you something?" she asked.

"Shoot," Samantha said.

"The girl in the purple dress..." Adriana began. Samantha made an annoyed sound.

"Not you too," she complained.

"Not me too…what?" Adriana inclined her head forward to inquire.

"Don't tell me you're one of her legion of fans," Samantha said.

"Not really. I just wondered what her relationship was to Dean Wesson," Adriana said.

"Tuh," Samantha exhaled her face reddening. "Relationship indeed," she said bitterly.

Adriana just looked at her; she knew that the best way to get information out of people was to keep silent and let them fill it.

"She's an attention whore who stole my boyfriend," Samantha said. "She seduced him with her differences and turned his head, taking advantage of the fact that he was freaking out about taking the helm at the family firm."

Adriana thought it sounded very much like a story Samantha told herself to soothe her wounded ego but she wasn't about to say so.

She looked thoughtfully at Dean; so he liked that dark meat did he? That might work to her advantage. She was here for the long game and once he tired of his little rebellion with lil miss sunshine over there…

"That's too bad," she said in encouragement.

"I can't wait for the day he comes crawling back," Samantha said smugly. "He'll have to really work for my forgiveness."

Adriana wanted to ask her if she really thought Dean would be coming back. Judging by the way he was wrapped around the new girl; he didn't seem to be missing her at all. She didn't think pointing that out would earn her any brownie points so she kept her mouth shut.

"Men," she said instead.

"Yeah," Samantha said smiling at her in shared commiseration. "Can't live with them, can't kill them."

Adriana laughed obligingly and then walked away. She had a lot to think about.

*****

"We would like to thank everyone for coming tonight," Jan Van der Roodt said in his vote of thanks and then announced how many millions had been raised for the victims of the Blood Diamond trade to raucous applause. He then wished everyone a lovely evening and announced that they were free to leave at their leisure.

Daniel came up to Meaghan and Dean as they sat talking at their tables, heads close together.

"Hey girlfriend, you haven't danced with me tonight," he said holding out his hand. Meaghan looked at Dean for permission to leave him and then smiled and reached out to take Daniel's proffered hand.

"So this has been fun," she ventured.

"It hasn't been too bad", he shrugged.

"Hey, Bain brought you to a function where his friends, colleagues, peers and family are in attendance. It's a good day."

"He hasn't danced with me once," Daniel said sadly.

"I think that's more about him than you. Just being here with you is a statement, you know? He probably didn't want to bombard people's faces with your over the top gayness," she consoled.

"There are other homosexuals in this room," Daniel pointed out.

"Maybe. But one thing I learned pretty fast in this life is that you can never compare your situation to other people's situations. That way lies madness," she advised Daniel.

"I know that. And normally I don't even think about it – but normally Bain doesn't treat me like just another friend he happened to bring to the event and not his boyfriend," Daniel's piercing gray eyes were shiny with unshed tears.

"You'll get there Danny; I promise you – you will," Meaghan said making a mental note to give Bain a piece of her mind.

"I know," he said but not like he meant it. He looked down at her with a pained smile. "I'm so glad we have you to talk to."

Meaghan smiled back at him. "We've both had crazy evenings; it hasn't been easy to maneuver with all the crazy that's been going on. I think we should probably not do too much thinking right now."

"You're probably right," Daniel said but he still sounded miserable. "When he goes home, he'll probably want some."

Meaghan stared at him, "You say that like you have no choice but to give it to him."

Daniel shrugged.

Meaghan glared at him, "Look Danny, Bain is my friend and I know you're not saying he would force you-"

"Of course he wouldn't force me. It's just he would expect –"

"God Danny don't tell me you feel like if he wants then you have to. I mean...you're a guy; you weren't even socialized that way."

Daniel laughed softly and looked down. "I guess...sometimes...I feel like Bain is this...amazing architect, great all around guy, sensitive, generous; and what am I except good looking? If I don't sleep with him then what good am I to him?"

"Jeez Danny low self esteem much?" Meaghan exclaimed in genuine distress. "Please don't tell me Bain told you that."

"He didn't. he wouldn't," Daniel grimaced. "I guess these are old hang ups. My own shit. I need to take care of it myself."

"You really do Danny because you're one of the most wonderful people I've ever met and if you were straight or I was a gay man, I'd totally fight Bain for you so don't you go saying that all you're good for is looking good," Meaghan chided.

"Don't let Dean hear you say that," Daniel smirked.

"I don't care if he does; it's true. You are great and you need to believe that."

"Thanks girlfriend," Daniel said with a shy smile.

"No. Thank you Danny for being exactly the guy Bain needs in his life. Never doubt your importance to him…or to me," she pressed.

Daniel just looked down, the smile playing on his lips like he wasn't really aware it was there. Meaghan leaned forward so she could look into his eyes.

"You believe me right?" she asked.

He looked up to meet her honey brown eyes with his piercing gray ones, "Yes."

Chapter 14

They got home at 4am, what with the various goodbyes that took the form of conversations that just couldn't wait. Bain and Meaghan made a date to hold a post mortem on Monday since Sunday was definitely blocked off for sleeping in and recovery. Meaghan made a point of telling Bain to treat Daniel like a lady and he responded with guilty agreement and a meaning-loaded glance that let her know that Daniel would feature prominently in their post party breakdown. Smith made a point of kissing her on both cheeks in the French manner and expressing his happiness that she'd come for the do within hearing of his parents and Poppy's mother. He even went so far as to introduce her to Jonathon Winchester, his father. His mother drifted off strategically before he could introduce her as well. Bella smiled from the sidelines in her fiancé's arms and gave her a side shrug as if to say, "What else could you expect?"

If someone were to ask Meaghan directly she would say that she would expect a little civility. I mean it was like these people were so used to getting their own way in everything that the slightest glitch in their plans led to epic sulking. I mean hadn't they ever heard of 'man proposes, God disposes'?

There were some cameramen outside the museum, waiting on guests to depart so they could take photos. Perhaps they were paparazzi, who knew? There were some celebrities among them after all, it would make sense that the paps would want to take pics. Meaghan wondered if she should shrink into the background while the cameras were snapping but Dean wound his arm around her and pulled her close, so Meaghan figured that he didn't mind. He even paused on the step with her so that the cameramen could take as many pictures of them as they wanted. Meaghan tried not to worry if she was displaying her good side or not or whether her dress was draped right or what people would say about her when they saw the picture but it was hard not to.

"Who's the girl?"

"Are you going steady?"

"What happened between you and Samantha Crawford?"

"Is it serious?"

The questions followed them as the cameras flashed and photographers ran after them. Dean mostly just ignored them and ushered Meaghan forward. Microphones were thrust in her face as people asked her questions. She knew intellectually that Dean was a handsome young billionaire and so inevitably people were interested in his love life but this was the first time she'd come face to face with public interest; right in her face and she maybe wasn't enjoying it as much as people might think she might. She just hoped she didn't trip and fall or hit her head on one of the ubiquitous microphones. Suddenly, they turned a corner and there was no-one surrounding them except other guests waiting for their cars. There must be some invisible velvet rope whose threshold they'd just crossed.

"Let's go home," Dean whispered in her ear and she nodded her agreement. He took her hand and led her through the throngs to where the valet was waiting with their car keys.

*****

Adriana watched them go with a considerable amount of chagrin. Dean had barely exchanged two personal words with her this evening and she was...displeased. She needed to do something to ramp up his interest levels but she currently had no idea what. Jan came to stand next to her.

"I think you should give up the dream of becoming Mrs. Dean Wesson, Ad," he said.

"Why would I do that?" she asked him.

"Maybe because he's clearly completely besotted with that black girl," Jan said.

"For now," Adriana said.

Jan turned to smile at her, "Oh Adriana, clearly you've never seen a man in love."

Adriana frowned at him, "That's shows how much you know. It's a rebound relationship."

Jan laughed, "Shows how much *you* know. He left his girlfriend of *fifteen years* for this one. You don't do that unless you got bit bad."

Adriana stared at him in stupefaction and then back at the duo as they got in Dean's vehicle. Her face fell so comically that Jan couldn't help doubling over with laughter. "If you hurry though, I'm sure you can snag some other billionaire. I saw quite a few people checking you out tonight," he teased.

Adriana flipped him off and then went off in search of her own car.

Time for plan B.

*****

Meaghan flopped on the couch and put her feet up on the coffee

table, waiting for Dean to stop pottering about checking security

settings, light switches, anything he could find to stall this talk.

Meaghan let him delay the inevitable as much as he could, amusing

herself by imagining the next thing he'd find to do. At last resort he

could always whip up a pot of coffee.

"Coffee?" he asked her right on cue.

She laughed to herself before nodding her head and he went to the

kitchen to watch over the coffeemaker as the coffee came to boil.

Clearly it couldn't do it without his supervision. Meaghan adjusted

herself to be the most comfortable on the soft leather couch and

put on CNN. Perhaps she could create some perspective by

watching really bad news – like that disappearing Malaysian plane or the war in Ukraine. Heavy stuff which really mattered as opposed to a few lies and omissions by her darling boyfriend.

Dean walked in with the coffee and placed her cup carefully in front of her. It was brimming with cream and he'd clearly taken his time to do it just right for her. She decided to award him ten points for that. Since lying was like minus a thousand points it really wasn't much but it was something. Dean picked up the remote and changed the channel to a music channel instead. A black girl with flaming red hair was running through a field as she sang in a fiery contralto;

Want you to MAKE ME FEEL!

Like I'm the only girl in the WOORLLD!

Like I'm the only one that you'll ever LOOOVE!

Like I'm the only one who holds your HEARRRT!

Only Girl in the World

Meaghan could totally relate. What girl didn't want to feel like that? She turned her attention back to Dean, and drew a breath. Time to get to business.

"So," she said and picked up her coffee to taste. It was perfectly made and she added another five points for attention to detail.

"So," Dean repeated.

"Why did you lie to me about the recreation center?" she asked at once.

"I didn't lie," he protested at once. "I just didn't tell you."

"Why?" Meaghan asked.

Dean looked off into the distance. "I always feel like that's the wrong question. Isn't that what they say in therapy? The why question is the wrong one?"

"Are you going to stall all night? Because if so I'd much rather just go to sleep and break up with you in the morning."

Dean smiled. "If you weren't my girlfriend; if you were just maybe someone I knew who happened to work at this foundation whose project I was funding, would you expect that I would tell you about this?" he asked.

"Of course not. But I'm not just Jane Public here. I *am* your girlfriend," she said, sounding a little more intense than maybe she intended.

"Yes you are, but you're also an employee and if you knew that your boyfriend was funding this project would it have made you maybe, self-conscious at work? Maybe feel like every compliment is because of what I was doing? Maybe that I was trying to buy you a better job?"

Meaghan thought about it trying to imagine herself in that situation. "I don't think I'm that insecure," she said at last.

"Okay maybe not but it wouldn't have raised questions in your mind?" Dean persisted.

Meaghan sat back eyes narrowed, she was silent for a long while, thinking.

"Correct me if I'm wrong, but it sounds to me like you woke up and decided for me how you thought I'd react to something and on that basis or not, you decide for me, whether or not I should know something that concerns me directly?" she said.

Dean went over her words, trying to find a loophole but closed his eyes finally. "Yes," he said.

"I see," Meaghan said.

"Meaghan listen-" Dean began to say.

"No, you listen Dean Wesson; I do not know who you think you are but you do not *ever* decide what is good for me or what I should think or do or *anything*!" she said.

"Okay. I'm sorry," Dean said.

"No!" Meaghan snarled. "You don't get to say sorry and expect forgiveness."

"Why not?" Dean asked.

"Because...this is a new low and I'm not just going to dismiss it and say it's okay because it's not."

Dean's face became very serious. "I do understand what you're saying and in the spirit of being completely honest I'm going to tell you the real reason why I didn't tell you."

Meaghan stared at him in surprise, she hadn't expected a curve ball.

"The real reason?" she asked.

"Yes. The real reason," Dean said his face solemn.

"Okay. Hit me," Meaghan said.

"I was...I won't say jealous because that's not the word and it implies that I still have questions or don't trust you which is just not true. I do trust you, completely. I think that I've come to trust you more than anyone else in my life because you're just so upfront with me; the good and the bad."

"Okay," Meaghan said at a loss as to how to react to this.

"And I say the good and the bad but honestly what you consider "bad" is just really cute to me and I don't feel like I should contaminate you with my darkness."

"What darkness?" Meaghan scoffed.

"That's another thing about you. You see me in this like...great light and I don't want to tarnish that," he said sadly.

"You won't," Meaghan assured him gently. "Just tell me already."

"So I know you say he's just your supervisor, your colleague and your boss. But I've seen how he looks at you; the way his eyes light up. I know that look. It's familiar, I see it in the mirror every day, every time I think of you."

Meaghan looked away.

"No. Don't look away," Dean said and Meaghan looked back at him.

"I don't trust him, and I think he's interested in more than a professional relationship with you. So don't get me wrong. We did the due diligence, we passed it by the board, got their approval. I'm the one who proposed it of course; just seeing the way your eyes light up when you talk about making a difference in those lives...I mean we've had a foundation for as long as I've been alive, possibly longer. But we don't do hands on," he said.

Meaghan inclined her head to the side and sighed. Dean knew he was being long-winded but he wanted her to understand.

"So yeah, I proposed that we fund the recreation center that Conrad's foundation needs and the board approved it and I volunteered to liaise between their foundation and ours because I was familiar with the players...but really I did it so I could keep an eye on him. Make sure he didn't try anything. It's not that I don't trust you Meaghan, you have to believe that."

"I do," Meaghan said.

"It's just that I'm maybe a little more jealous and possessive than I have let on," Dean finished sheepishly.

Meaghan stared at him in stupefaction. Then she laughed and laughed and laughed. "I quite literally do not know what to say," she said between chortles.

"Say you forgive me," Dean said a tentative smile spreading over his face.

"No," Meaghan said shortly.

"Come on Megs. Please?" Dean begged.

"No," Meaghan repeated.

"What do I have to do? I came clean with no prompting. I could have just shut up about the jealous possessive shit," he bargained.

"That's true," Meaghan conceded. "But I can't condone your Cro Magnon behavior because you were honest with me."

"What if I promise not to be such a Neanderthal?" Dean asked.

"Actions speak louder," Meaghan declared.

"Fine you can have me on double secret probation until I prove that I can behaved like an evolved human being."

"Deal," Meaghan said holding out her hand to shake.

Dean looked at it and then up at her face. "Really, we're regressing to hand shakes now? What happened to kissing?"

"You do like to push it don't you?" she said.

"Hey, I'm not a billionaire by accident," Dean said.

Meaghan opened her mouth to point out that most of that wealth was inherited, but then she thought about all the effort he'd put into keeping the company stable when his father had his stroke and closed it again.

"So come on lets kiss and make up," Dean said.

"We can do that, but don't think you're off the hook," Meaghan warned.

"I won't," Dean said leaning forward with his eyes on her lips.

"Wait," Meaghan said and Dean drew back immediately. "I need to get out of this dress first. It's rented."

"Not anymore," Dean said.

"Excuse me?" Meaghan asked.

"You look lovely in it, no way you're giving that back," Dean said.

"There you go again with the pre-historic shit," Meaghan said.

"Sorry. Let me rephrase. Please allow me to purchase that garment on your behalf because it looks really lovely on you and my heart would be broken to see you return something that was clearly made for you."

"Pretty pretty words," Meaghan mocked.

"Do they have the desired effect?" Dean asked.

Meaghan shrugged. "Well I guess you *are* right about one thing; this dress was made for me," she said making Dean laugh.

"And I guess it would be churlish of me to refuse to let you pay for it," she continued.

"Really churlish," Dean agreed.

"So okay, you can buy me the dress," she said.

"And the shoes, the handbag and most especially the bobby pin in your hair?" he asked eagerly.

"You just can't help yourself can you?"

"I really can't," Dean agreed.

Meaghan just shook her head and laughed.

"While you're in an agreeable mood..." Dean said after a long silence.

"I'm in an agreeable mood?" Meaghan asked in surprise.

"Yes, you are," Dean informed. "So while it lasts, I might as well ask you; how would you feel about living together?"

"What?!?" Meaghan exclaimed completely taken by surprise. She knew from all the books on 'handling men' that the man never asked to progress the relationship without some sort of prompting from the woman...more like manipulation. Dean was going completely off book. This was unacceptable?

"I said, how would you feel about living together?" he repeated.

Meaghan stared off into the middle distance. "I don't know; this place is a little far from my work," she hedged.

"Yeah, I mean of course we'd have to find a bigger place somewhere more central to both of our workstations. Or maybe I can get you a vehicle so you can get anywhere from anywhere," Dean suggested.

"Whoa. Slow down," Meaghan said.

"Why?" Dean asked.

Meaghan opened her mouth and then looked around for a bit, searching for inspiration. "You seem to have thought about this a lot," she said at last.

"Its been floating around in my head for a while," he admitted. "Are you saying you've never thought about it?"

"What? Living together? How could I think about that when your mother doesn't even acknowledge my existence. It's like a stonewall blocking any thoughts of the future," she said and then caught sight of his face and hastened to add, "Not that I'm blaming you or even her it's just that these are the facts."

Dean sighed. "Okay eliminating all the bottlenecks, have you thought about me and you, maybe living together, maybe... someday...more than that?"

"Yes, I've thought about it. Of course I have. More like in the guise of a fantasy. Us living in a two story house with a garden and a dog and beautiful blended children running around causing havoc and

not getting shot by the cops…"Meaghan smiled but Dean didn't.

"Do you want that?" he asked instead.

"Of course I do Dean," she said but with resignation in her tone.

"Doesn't mean I'm gonna get it."

"Why not?" Dean asked staring intently into her eyes.

Meaghan shook her head at him, "How are we going to do it,

outside of fantasy land I mean?"

"Say yes. Say yes to moving in with me and I'll show you how we do

it," he said taking both her hands in his.

Meaghan stared at him for a long time and then leaned forward

and placed her lips on his. She ran her tongue over his lips and he

responded by parting his lips and letting her in. Their lips mashed

together as they tasted each other, bodies straining to get closer.

Dean took hold of her hair in his fists, pushing her face into his mouth and then pulled back, staring at her.

"What was that for?" he asked.

"Hey, you're the one who said that deals are sealed with a kiss," she said making Dean smile quite giddily.

"Oh yaass!" he exclaimed with joy. "So you're saying that's a yes."

Meaghan pretended to hold an ear piece to her ear while holding up a finger for Dean to shush. "Let me check with the fans," she said pretending to talk into a speaker.

"And the results are coming in and we can confirm that it is a yes," she said.

Dean's smile lit up his whole face, "Best decision you ever made."

The end... but there's more:

If you enjoyed this ebook and want me to keep writing more, please leave a review of it on the store where you bought it. By doing so you'll allow me more time to write these books for you as they'll get

more exposure. So thank you. :)

Get Free Romance eBooks!

Hi there. As a special thank you for buying this book, for a limited

time I want to send you some great ebooks completely **free of**

charge directly to your email! You can get it by going to this page:

www.saucyromancebooks.com/physical

You can see a the cover of these books on the next page:

www.SaucyRomanceBooks.com/RomanceBooks

ONE LONE COWBOY, ONE WOMAN ON A MISSION...

THE LONE COWBOY

EMILY J

ROCHELLE

IF IT'S MEANT TO BE... *Him*

KIMBERLY GREENFORD

...IRE MET HIS MATCH?

UCH LASS

...ILDING

PLAYERS GONNA PLAY?

SHE'S THE ONE HE WANTS BUT CAN SHE TRUST HIM?

ONE VAMPIRE. ONE COP. ONE LOVE.

VAMPIRES OF CLEARVIEW

J A FIELDING

These ebooks are so exclusive you can't even buy them. When you download them I'll also send you updates when new books like this are available.

Again, that link is:

www.saucyromancebooks.com/physical

Now, if you enjoyed the book you just read, please leave a positive review of it where you bought it (e.g. Amazon). It'll help get it out there a lot more and mean I can continue writing these books for you. So thank you. :)

More Books By Cher Etan

Enjoyed that? Well this is just part 2 in the series. You can see other parts here:

1. When We Meet Again.

2. Make Me Yours.

Search those on Amazon followed by 'Cher Etan'.

You can also see other related books by myself and other top romance authors at:

www.saucyromancebooks.com/romancebooks

When We Meet Again Sample

The book you just read is part 2 in the series. Part 1, 'When We Meet Again' can be sampled below:

"Meaghan!" her mother called as she came in to the trailer at 6am, "are you awake? If you hurry, Mr. Henley can give you a lift to the bus stop. He's headed out in ten."

Meaghan pushed the curtain that acted as a partition to her sleeping space aside, "I'm dressed and ready Mama," she said with a smile. Her mother smiled back at her and flopped on the sofa in exhaustion. The night shift at the hospital really took it out of her sometimes. All the emergencies seemed to happen then.

"How was work?" Meaghan asked.

"Great. We had four GSWs and it wasn't even the same shoot out. One was a woman who was shot by her husband because she was walking out on him. Two teenagers looked gang-related and one middle-aged guy; shot by the police."

Meaghan flinched in sympathy and her mom nodded her response.

"Yeah, and that was the fun part. There was the diabetic going into insulin shock because of too many missed meals, and that HIV positive mom who comes in for checkups turned up with jaundice. Fun times."

"Wow mom, I do not know how you do it," Meaghan said as she gathered her school books together.

www.SaucyRomanceBooks.com/RomanceBooks

"Frankly my dear, neither do I. I'm off to shower and sleep now so do you need anything?"

"I'm fine Mama," Meaghan said leaning up to kiss her mother as she passed on her way out. Her mother waved and wished her a good day and then she was off to the shower. Meaghan could see how tired she was. In addition to working full time as a nurse at the general hospital, her mother also worked part time at the grocery store as a clerk. She made barely enough to make ends meet and Meaghan knew that; which was why she was applying for academic assistance to attend Dalton School. She'd taken her test for the interview and had just received the notification that she'd passed and had been awarded a place. Now all she had to do was convince them that she qualified for one of their scholarships. She was ready to work extra hard on this if they would just agree to pay her tuition and maybe give her a small stipend for books. If they agreed with her, *then* she could tell her mother. She knew how much it would break her mother's heart if she knew that her daughter wanted to attend a school that she couldn't pay for. So there was no use in getting both their hopes up. She'd try for the scholarship, if she succeeded then yay. If she failed...well mother would never have to know she'd even applied.

Mr. Henley was waiting for her leaning on his semi as he smoked a cigarette. He smiled when he saw her approach and walked to his door, getting into the truck and pulling open the passenger door for her. Classic rock was already blasting from the speakers of his stereo. Mr. Henley had infected her with his penchant for rock music from the eighties. He had everything from AC/DC to Bon Jovi and he not only introduced her to it, but was always picking up both CDs and Vinyl for her when he went on his trips. She figured that she liked the music so much because listening to it gave her a chance to use her late father's record player that he'd bequeathed to her. And Mr. Henley was right; the music really did sound better on vinyl.

They talked about the possibility of seeing U2 in concert when they came to town in a few weeks. Mr. Henley thought that he could maybe get tickets but Meaghan couldn't really afford to buy concert tickets and she wouldn't take one for free. Mr. Henley tried to make it seem like she'd be doing him a favor if she agreed to go with him but Meaghan's mama had taught her that there was no such thing as a free lunch. Mr. Henley was nice and all but it just didn't pay to put any ideas in his head. And going out to a rock concert with him was crossing the line...not that she'd ever seen any evidence that he was into pedophilia or anything but best to be safe rather than sorry.

"Mr. Henley it's really nice of you to offer but my mama wouldn't like for me to go out with you like that on my own so I can't. I'm sorry," she said.

"Well how about I just give you the ticket and you go on your own?" he wheedled.

Meaghan thought about it, "No. I can't go on my own, I'm not old enough and I still can't pay for the ticket."

Mr. Henley sighed, "Fine then. I'll just have to record it for you on my video camera. It's not the same as seeing it live though."

"I know," Meaghan said wistfully, "and I really really wish I could go but I can't."

"Hey. What if they're not free? What if you…wash my trailer for me for a month as exchange?" Mr. Henley suggested, very excited at his brilliant compromise.

Meaghan smiled to see him so excited, "I can't Mr. Henley. I still wouldn't be able to go because I can't go alone."

"And you won't let me take you," he sighed in disappointment and was so preoccupied with their conversation that he almost passed the bus stop, "Fine then. It's your funeral," he said as he let her out.

"Bye Mr. Henley," Meaghan said with a small wave.

"You have a good day Miss Sunshine," he replied with a smile of his own and drove off into the sunrise.

There were some other kids from her school waiting for the bus as well and they greeted her casually but then went back to their conversation. Meaghan was a bright student and she was an apt pupil but that didn't mean she knew how to win friends and influence people. Being an only child and living more as roommates and friends with her mom rather than traditional mother and daughter meant that she was used to having conversations that didn't begin with "Like..."

She also had a very clear picture of what she wanted her future to look like and was laser focused on that. It didn't leave her a lot in common with her classmates. Meaghan didn't mind though. She had all the friends she needed in Mr. Henley and her mother.

The school bus drew up and the driver got the door open, giving Meaghan a grin. He always grinned at her; he had told her one time that her hair reminded him of Donna Summer in her prime. Meaghan hadn't known who that was so she'd gone to look her up on yahoo. Looking at the great halo of Donna Summer's hair in a picture she'd found, she nodded her agreement. Yeah, she could see how the giant pouf she wore her hair in would remind Clarence of this music star. And she was also a tall girl; willowy. The only discordant note was the glasses she wore and her braces. She decided to take it as a compliment. Meaghan had always been a glass half full type of person.

Ms. Lainey was waiting for her as the bus drew up at the school.

She was instrumental in helping Meaghan apply to Dalton School

and today they needed to prep for the interview that would

determine whether or not she got that scholarship. They only had

thirty minutes before class began and the interview was at lunch

hour. It would have to be enough.

*****

"Come in Meaghan Leonard is it? Don't be scared," the severe

looking lady with the tortoise shell glasses said. There was a panel

of three people; the severe lady, a pale fat gentleman in a black suit

and a pin striped lawyer type with a pince nez. Meaghan wasn't

afraid but a lot was riding on this interview and a lot of thought

went into every step she took. That might have made her appear a

bit tentative but Meaghan wasn't sure that was entirely a bad thing.

Might make at least one of these panelists sympathetic. As long as

she was articulate and convincing. Meaghan prayed that she would be convincing enough. Heaven knew there were enough people waiting to take her place if she wasn't.

"You applied to this school to join our high school next year did you not?" severe woman asked. The other two panelists were just staring at her.

"Yes I did," she replied nodding her head once. In honor of the occasion, she'd tied her hair in a tight bun at the back of her head. Ms. Lainey had helped her with the style; she'd said it made her look more serious.

"And you passed and have been accepted?" Severe asked her again.

"Yes ma'am," she replied, nodding again.

"So please tell us in your own words why you feel you qualify for this scholarship?" the lady asked her. Meaghan took a deep breath and began to speak.

Her father had died in the first Iraq war; he had been an army medic who died when the camp was bombed by friendly fire. They received his small military pension but it was barely enough to keep them clothed. Her mother worked two jobs as a nurse and a store clerk to provide for them but there was definitely no money for private school. Meaghan had been a good student consistently throughout her formative years as well as an active participant in student politics. She worked as a photographer for the school newspaper and a photograph of hers had been used by the local papers. She aspired to be a surgeon and she knew that Dalton was a stepping stone that could get her where she needed to be. She asked nicely for their consideration and pledged to work hard to ensure that if they chose her they would be vindicated in that choice. She thanked them nicely for taking the time to interview her and listen to her.

By the time she was finished fat pasty looking guy was actually looking interested in the proceedings. She wondered why they didn't introduce themselves. Perhaps they didn't want her to have their names in case they rejected her bid...

*****

It was the final day of exams when Ms. Lainey asked her to stay behind after all her classmates had filed out. She looked grim and Meaghan braced herself for news that was maybe not good. She began to think what her plan B could be; public high schools might not be an automatic in to an Ivy League school, nevertheless, it wasn't impossible.

"Meaghan, I just received a reply from the panel at Dalton. I haven't opened the letter. I thought we could do it together," Ms. Lainey said. Meaghan could barely find the wherewithal to nod her head. She swallowed hard; suddenly her mouth was really dry. Had she gotten in?

www.SaucyRomanceBooks.com/RomanceBooks

Ms. Lainey slit open the envelope and pulled out the letter.

"Dear Ms. Leonard, we are pleased to offer you-"

That's as far as Ms. Lainey got before Meaghan was screaming and crying in her arms, her joy could hardly be contained. She snatched the letter to read the words for herself. They were offering her the scholarship as well as a book stipend. Furthermore, transportation to and from school was part of the package. Meaghan's heart was so full she felt it was leaking out of her through her eyes. She looked up at Ms. Lainey; it looked like she was leaking at the eyes too.

"You should go and tell your mother," she said to Meaghan.

Meaghan nodded mutely and ran out of the door, forgetting her bag behind her.

*****

When Meaghan began high school, she had all these lofty ideas of

how Dalton School would be. She imagined herself having debates

on history, culture and politics with her classmates and teachers but

she quickly learned one thing. School kids were the same

everywhere and teachers were more concerned with homework

turned in on time than abstract debates on subjects beyond their

ability to do anything about. So just like in middle school, Meaghan

found herself spending more and more time in the library; among

books which were always ready to engage her in her hunger for

knowledge and higher truths. She took to spending her spare time

in there, reading everything that caught her eye. The Dalton library

was certainly extensive. She didn't have as much time to utilize it as

she would like; as soon as she turned sixteen she began work at Mr.

Henley's garage; keeping his records in order after school. She liked

the job because it taught her a lot about managing finances on a

tight budget, plus Mr. Henley didn't mind if she read her books on

her breaks. The perpetual rock music playing in the background was also another plus. She was working for a boss she liked, in a job she enjoyed and surrounded by her favorite music. She couldn't ask more from life.

*****

She was working late one night, or rather she'd gotten caught up reading the Iliad while Bon Jovi blasted from the speakers and she didn't want to move when a new customer drove into the garage. She peered down from the window in the office and saw that the garage was deserted. Mr. Henley had said something about going out for a smoke; no smoking was allowed in the garage because it was a fire hazard and it was late so no-one else seemed to be around. She wondered what she should do; it wasn't like she could help the customer with his car...

He alighted from the vehicle and Meaghan got a load of his full head of hair as he looked around for someone to help him. He looked lost. The car was too expensive for this neighborhood and the guy was too well dressed. Meaghan stood and left the office, descending the stairs self-consciously as the guy watched her come to him. She guessed there was nothing else to look at really but still she wished he would look away.

"Hi. Can I help you?" she asked him. Now that she was up close to him and standing on the same level she could see how tall he was; and well built. But not as old as she'd first thought when she saw his clothes. No, he was closer to her age than the mid twenties she'd assumed at his outfit. Fitted khaki slacks and blue fitted shirt that looked tailor made for him. His dark hair was windswept and untidy but that could have been because he'd just alighted from a convertible...Lamborghini Aventador if she wasn't mistaken. His green eyes were so intent on her that she felt like squirming but drew herself up instead and looked back at him.

"Where do I know you from?" he asked ignoring her question.

"What? I'm pretty sure I don't know you," she replied and then wondered if that was rude and if Mr. Henley would be mad at her for being brusque with his customers.

"Yes. I've seen you somewhere," he said looking her up and down. And then his eyes fell on the book in her hand. It was emblazoned with 'The Dalton School' along its sleeve which was facing him. The frown cleared from his face.

"Oh you're the scholarship chick in my biological science class aren't you?" he asked. "You look different without the mountain of books you're usually carrying." Meaghan stared at him in stupefaction.

"What?" she asked completely stymied by the fact that not only did this guy actually know her but that he remembered her from school? She'd been feeling practically invisible at Dalton. Apart from her friend Bainbury (call me Bain he always said- something about Batman) who she'd met in her elective creative writing course, she had been pretty sure no-one else in the school even knew she

existed. She wasn't even important enough to bully.

"Yeah. You sit in the front and your hand is always up even when

the teacher hasn't really asked a question," he said smirking

slightly. If Meaghan had been any lighter skinned she'd be blushing

but even so she felt her cheeks grow hot.

"Oh er, well that notwithstanding, how can I help you at this

moment?" she asked him.

"Are you a mechanic?" he asked, "I need a mechanic."

"Mr. Henley will be back shortly if you'd like to wait for him," she

replied.

"Thanks, I will," he said. Meaghan stared at him, wondering what to

say now.

"Er what happened?" she asked.

"What happened?" the guy echoed.

"To your car," Meaghan clarified wondering if she should have started with an introduction. The guy seemed to hesitate so Meaghan jumped in.

"I'm Meaghan by the way," she said stretching out her hand to shake. The guy looked skeptically at it.

"Dean," he said reaching out to shake her hand reluctantly.

"Good to meet you Dean. Are you alright? Your car looks pretty banged up – did you escape unhurt," she asked briskly so he would answer without thinking too much about it.

Dean looked at his car and then at her, "Er well, I think I might have hurt my ribs a bit but otherwise I'm fine. I just need the car fixed really fast so my dad doesn't need to find out about this," he said.

At that point, Mr. Henley stepped inside so Dean and he could talk and come to some agreement. Dean was apparently willing to pay extra if Mr. Henley could repair the car within the night. The side of the car was pretty banged up and normally Mr. Henley would turn down such a deal but Dean was offering twice his normal rate.

"Fine. Let me see what I can do," he said. Dean heaved a sigh of relief and stepped aside so Mr. Henley could assess the damage. Meaghan stepped closer to him and looked up at him shyly.

"If you want, I can take a look at your injuries and see if I can do anything."

"Oh. Are you a medic now too?" Dean's tone was just this side of nasty.

"I'm trained in first aid," Meaghan replied neutrally. Dean continued to look at her then seemed embarrassed at his behavior because he dipped his head and stammered slightly.

"Er yeah if you don't mind," he mumbled.

She led him up to Mr. Henley's office and retrieved the first aid kit from underneath the sink in the bathroom.

"You'll need to remove your shirt," she said quietly. Dean smirked and made a show of removing his shirt in a slow and sexy way, unbuttoning slowly and then inching it off his body with slow careful movements that showed off his chiseled physique to full effect. Meaghan was diverted until she saw the bruised swelling that ran all the way from his sternum down to his hipbone. It looked like it hurt quite a bit and Meaghan gasped in sympathy. Dean glanced downward to see what he was looking at and his face blanched but he recovered quite quickly and he shrugged nonchalantly.

"It's nothing; barely hurts," he said.

Meaghan turned toward the door, "Stay there, I have some ointment in my trailer that will help with the bruising and the swelling," she said and then dashed out and left him staring after her in bemusement.

Her trailer wasn't far and she was back before long clutching a container of homemade ointment that contained some aloe vera, valerian root, willow bark, ginger and propolis. It was good for swelling, bleeding and had antibiotic properties as well as being a painkiller. If Dean wanted to keep this accident under the radar then he very likely wouldn't be visiting a hospital. Best to cover all bases.

His shirt was still off and he was sitting on the edge of the desk as if he belonged there. Meaghan came close and put the jar down, running her hand lightly over his bruises trying to get a sense of how bad they were. He didn't flinch but he was holding his breath the entire time her hands were on him.

"Does this hurt?" she asked softly. Mutely he shook his head. She went to the sink to get some hot water in a bowl and gently dabbed his side with it. Then she took the ointment and gently dabbed it on as well. She could see him trying to regulate his breathing as she did so and did her best not to hurt him.

"There. All done," she said after she was through.

"Thank you," Dean said

"You're very welcome", Meaghan replied and stepped back. "Can I get you something to drink maybe?"

Dean smirked at her again, "Ever the gracious host." He said teasingly, "Sure I could drink a coke if you have it."

Meaghan nodded and went down to the coke dispenser in the lobby. She had a few coins in her hand that she used to get him a coke. She didn't know why she was bothering with all this for this guy who clearly wasn't too impressed with her anyway. For all she knew she'd never see him again after tonight. But no, wait, apparently they were in the same class.

Meaghan carried the can of coke upstairs and gave it to him. He took it with a nod of thanks and drank it down almost in one fell swoop.

"So...you work here huh?" he asked her when he put the can down.

"Yes," she replied and then cast around for something else to say, "You didn't tell me what happened to your car."

"It's kind of private," Dean said.

"Right oh, sorry I didn't mean to pry," Meaghan backed up immediately. Dean grinned at her.

"Kidding. My girlfriend was drunk, she was driving; she banged into a telephone pole. Nobody was hurt in the making of this melodrama," he said.

"Except you," Meaghan said.

"Except me," Dean replied.

www.SaucyRomanceBooks.com/RomanceBooks

"Sorry about that," Meaghan ventured.

"No it's cool. That's what you get I guess."

"I would hope not. But your girlfriend's fine?"

"Still very drunk but safely asleep in her bed," Dean said.

Meaghan nodded her head, wondering at the shenanigans these rich kids got up to.

"Is that...Iliad you're reading?" Dean asked her sounding insultingly surprised.

"Yes," she bit out in preemptive self defense.

"I always found that Zeus was over-rated," Dean said in casual dismissal.

Meaghan couldn't help herself, she puffed up in indignation.

"What?" she cried. "What do you mean by over-rated. There is absolutely no way in this world or the next that Zeus can be over-

rated."

"Oh yeah," Dean rose to the challenge. "Well let me count the

ways", he said lifting up his hand in the air to do a verbal

countdown.

The time flew past as they argued over the Iliad and its implications

for modern life and what Homer had said as opposed to what he

meant and before they knew it, Dean's car was ready and it was

going on midnight. Meaghan needed to go home and get some

sleep. Luckily her mother was on night shift again so she might not

find out how late she'd actually gotten in. she bid Dean goodbye

and left after assuring him that she could get home by herself

perfectly safely.

48260326R00199

Made in the USA
Charleston, SC
30 October 2015